I0772740

Dedication

To my son Kevhan and my daughter Keira, thank you for your encouragement—you keep me going in my pursuit to be the best dad I can be. This story is my testament to the love I have for both of you

Forward

Already in 1998, I could have predicted that life would smile on the lively and dynamic young man I met one day in Cap-Haitian. Curious and intelligent, he seemed destined for business and politics. Twenty years later, by one of those curious coincidences of life, I found myself in New York, facing a man who had become mature and successful in Uncle Sam's country. Nevertheless, he still bubbled with passion for his beloved native country, Haiti.

Realph Saintil once dreamed of serving his country and contributing to the emancipation of his people. He has achieved a remarkable feat by navigating the Haitian situation, drawing on his imagination to present us with "Money, Love and Power." This novel aspires to later bring its phantasmagorical vision to the big screen.

In a cosmopolitan setting that reflects his journey as a citizen of the world, Realph has brought forth dreams nurtured by an entire Haitian imagination. Drawing inexorably from the folklore of his fertile land, he offers us an innovative publication. Like the labyrinthine paths of a dream, let us enter with passion into the colorful universe of this novel, which is both script and film.

May the divine imagination of Realph Saintil transport us towards his light.

And there was light!

Ayibobo!

Jean-Daniel Lafontant

Forward

(In French)

Déjà en 1998, j'aurais pu prédire que la vie sourirait au jeune homme vif et dynamique que je rencontrai un jour au Cap-Haitien. Curieux et intelligent, il me parut destiné aux affaires et à la politique. 20 ans plus tard, par un de ces curieux hasard de la vie, je me suis retrouvé à New York face à celui qui était devenu un homme mur et couronné de succès dans le pays de l'oncle Tom. Néanmoins, il bouillonnait toujours de passion pour son cher pays natal, Haïti.

…Realph Saintil rèvait alors de servir son pays et contribuer à l'émancipation de son peuple. Il réussit un tour de force en conitournant la conjoncture Haïtienne, en puisant dans son imaginaire pour nous présenter

"Money, Love and Power". Ce roman ambitionne de plus tard mettre sur grand écran sa vision fantasmagorique….

Dans un cadre cosmopolite qui reflète son parcours de citoyen du monde, Realph a sorti de ses tripes des rêves bercés par tout un imaginaire haïtien. Puisant inexorablement dans le folklore de son terroir fertile, il nous propose une publication novatrice. Tel dans les méandres labyrinthiques d'un songe, rentrons avec passion dans l'univers coloré de ce roman à la fois script et film.

Que la divine imagination de Realph Saintil nous transporte vers sa lumière.

Et la lumière fut!

Ayibobo!

Jean-Daniel Lafontant

Money, Love and Power : A Testimony of Faith and Perseverance

Ifirst met Realph Saintil in my office in Brooklyn about fifteen years ago. From the very beginning, it was clear that he had come to New York with a mission, a divine purpose rooted in unwavering determination. His objective was not merely to move forward, but to rise, to break barriers, and to transform the Haitian community for the better.

Each time he came to see me, I saw in him the fire of a young man who refused to be confined by limitations. His heart was set on change, his mind on progress, and his spirit on the greater calling that God had placed upon his life.

Realph, I congratulate you not just for what you have accomplished, but for the man you are and the leader you have become. You are a beacon of hope, an instrument of transformation, and a testament to what faith, perseverance, and hard work can achieve.

I urge you to continue pressing forward. The road may be demanding, and the sacrifices many, but know this: by the grace of God, you will reach the heights He has destined for you. And your riches lie in your faith, your vision, and your relentless drive.

When the path ahead seems impossible, remember this: if your hands cannot reach it, step over a chair, climb a ladder, or find any means necessary to go higher. Never accepts the limiting mindset of Kwoke makout kote men kapab rive" the belief that one should only strive for what is within easy reach. That is the philosophy of those who settle. But you, Realph, are called to soar. Always aim higher, push further, and trust that the Lord will make a way where there seems to be none.

May God's favor be upon you. Keep climbing, keep believing, and keep striving, for we shall meet at the TOP!

Bishop Philius Nicolas

President of the Federation of Haitian Protestant Churches Overseas

Introduction

Money, **Love and Power** is a very deep and imaginative novel with broad appeal, as the author dwells on personalities and situations that people find themselves in during their lifetime. By injecting the surreal, even ethereal, into the story, he keeps one hooked, wanting to find out what's next. At times, one wonders whether it's all a dream, but the stark reality described makes one think otherwise.

Is the Nicky personality, who was close to his mom, that is introduced early on in the story, a "he" or a "she", for he/she appears to play both roles. Is that inherited from his/her Albino father? You decide. But when we find Nicky with his partner Marytza, to whom he got married, unquestionably he's playing the masculine role, and that continues to the end. When he got into a car accident that threatened his life, he's found at a hospital where Marytza tries her best to have him hold unto life. On her guitar, she plays melodies to soften his pain and lift up his spirit.

The Catholic priest Sebastian comes to visit Nicky at the hospital, as most people consider him on his deathbed. And the priest feels the allure of Marytza. There's a scene where it's mentioned that Sebastian was about to commit rape. But the "guardian angels" of Nicky and Marytza intervened in time. In fact, you'll find out that this couple "transcended the boundaries of mortal existence." The author asserts that they had "embraced the mysteries of the universe and found comfort in the presence of their guardian angels." In fact, Author Saintil maintains that, "With faith as their compass, they ventured into the unknown, ready to embrace whatever the future held." And the couple lived on till old age.

Needless to say, you are delving into a novel in which the spiritual and the physical worlds intersect. Indeed, there's much to learn. As the French saying goes: *"Bonne lecture!"* Enjoy!

Raymond Alcide Joseph*

Mr. Joseph, a former ambassador of Haiti to the United States, is co-founder of the Haiti-

Observateur, the first weekly for the Haitian diaspora, launched in New York, on July 23, 1971.

Preface
By Dan Whitman

Behind Every Life, a Story

"All wisdom is found in stories," said American novelist Verlin Cassill.

After 25 years of gestation, Realph Saintil's novel/movie treatment now hang glides between "reality," fantasy, the subconscious, moments that seem hallucinatory, and parable. Marked by yearning, loss, corresponding gain, his story finds resonance with any reader who has taken note of life's conundrums.

So, which is it, "reality" or dreams? Humans have yet to explain dreams, vivid in every person's sleep, quicky forgotten when "consciousness" returns. Shakespeare made light of it in *Midsummer Night's Dream*, Calderón de la Barca employed its mysteries as theatrical puns in *Vida es Sueño*, 1636. Dreams present urgent questions, but so far no one has even managed to formulate the question exactly. We take dreams as somehow reflecting a deeper conscience beyond what we "know." Their "meaning" evades us, gave Freud some fame but little guidance. All cultures puzzle over them.

Money, Love and Power begins with an abstraction clearly stated: "loyalty brings bad luck." This sets us up for a tract on philosophy disguised as fiction, alerts us to the sterility of Sartre's meanderings in *la Nausée* or *l'Âge de Raison*, or, even more taxing, Jostein Gaarder's Norwegian history-of-philosophy-disguised-as-fiction, *Sophie's World*, 1991. Not so, in *Money, Love and Power*, which reverts directly to a lively narrative after laying down the "paradox of loyalty." The latter serves as an underpinning of the story following, rather than the reverse. This is what fiction does at its best, revealing the flesh and bones of characters we come to know – in this case, Clara, Robert, "the woman," "the lady," and Marytza.

Saintil draws on cultural contexts including Western rationalism, Christianity in its abstract form, and free borrowings of African and Haitian ways of making sense of the world's cruel chaos. The characters are entrenched, in a sense trapped in these contradicting patterns. All seek in vain to answer a question: What is the nature of the unknown beyond the known? All cultures address these quests, none satisfies them entirely.

Example: the driving force of *procreation* as a primary instinct rising above wishes for security, food, power, sleep, or even Eros. The Western reader is adrift in this hierarchy of needs, which doesn't appear at all in Maslov's version. "Whence the overriding need to create children?" says the Westerner, who considers this drive more as consequence than objective. Does it make sense to add yet more humans to an already overpopulated Earth, afflicted with famine and resource scarcity? Eros and reproduction are not the same, after all. Hence Saintil's tale adds a cultural element to challenge Western myths and beliefs. Do strong human drives assure species survival or undermine it? No easy answers to that. Perhaps both, strange to say.

One woman, faced with sterility, permits her husband to sleep with other women. Another character sees her permission as "a betrayal beyond comprehension." Effective fiction presents ideas in opposition, then leads the reader to draw conclusions which may coincide with the author's, maybe not, but which enliven the imagination. An adopted girl is returned to her biological parents in a court proceeding. We can blame the judge for this harshly logical outcome but cannot fault him for indifference.

A prevailing theme in Saintil's novel is albinism, considered a curse in some African cultures, a source of wisdom and even miracles in others. This may appear silly to albinos themselves. Those I've known seem to want just to proceed, free of vilification or deification. Kinder societies allow them this, condemnably superstitious don't. Albinos did not choose their chromosomes to be above or beneath others. In fact they don't *choose* them at all. The straitjacket of their identities draws us to consider Oedipus, maybe also Dostoyevsky's Alyosha or Raskolnikov or Mushkin, defined at birth rather than through a life fashioned consciously. This is a dark vision of humans marked by luck of the draw. Western societies and cultures – especially Anglo-Saxon ones – seek to escape these traps which they see as "fatalism." Let the reader decide.

In this tale Nicky's mother goes to a church expecting a miracle. This seems far-fetched. Others would say, accept miracles as they happen, don't expect or seek them, and certainly not from a self-appointed man in white robes with no qualification to perform them.

Again, the reader is to experience, not judge. Strength of character draws us in, and this power to fascinate is what gives story-telling its power.

Weird things happen here: water at a baptism turns to blood - but is this any "crazier" than loaves and fishes? Water to wine? "The somber skies wept" – we would call this Romantic Fallacy, but it captures even as English Romantic poetry did. Marytza sleepwalks, lives in the subconscious and in dreams, an "astral nomad." Even Eros himself appears and offers Marytza flowers. The outcome is a syncretic amalgam of Hellenic myth, Western Christianity, African consciousness which long ago might have been elevated by observers to a state above "superstition."

Humans generally superimpose illogical fantasy on opaque reality; the exact articulations we call "culture." Saintil brings this to us as challenge and illumination, and with the skill to draw, not lead, the reader to independent conclusions and reactions. At this juncture we find the charm of *Money, Love and Power*.

Dan Whitman

Prologue & Acknowledgements

The impetus for writing this book is rooted in my deep commitment to the promotion and preservation of Haitian culture. Haiti stands as a unique fusion of influences—by race, we are African; by customs, French; and within the very fabric of our traditions, the enduring traces of the Taíno-Spanish heritage resonate. This intricate blend of identities and histories is not merely a backdrop; it is the essence of who we are as a people.

Haiti, a nation born from the fires of revolution, now finds itself at a crossroads of cultural unification and spiritual awakening. Here, the rich tapestry of African heritage intertwines seamlessly with the complex layers of European and indigenous influences. This convergence has forged a culture unlike any other, where the soul of Africa thrives, even as it is shaped by centuries of French and Spanish contact.

In Haiti, spirituality is not just practiced—it is lived. It is in the air we breathe, the rhythms we dance to, and the language we speak. All religions find a place in this land, yet through it all, Haitians remain undeniably and intrinsically Vodou. It is more than a religion; it is our history, our identity, and our resilience.

This book is a celebration of this unique cultural synthesis and spiritual depth, a testament to the indomitable spirit of the Haitian people. It is my hope that through these pages, the world will come to understand and appreciate the profound complexity and beauty of Haiti, a nation that, against all odds, continues to stand as a beacon of cultural and spiritual.

In fact, the story of Money, Love and Power was conceived in the early days of my teenage years, in the vibrant city of Cap-Haitian, Haiti. It was there, amidst the warmth of the Caribbean sun and the whispers of the sea, that my dreams began to take shape. Dreams that transcended the boundaries of reality, entwined with mystery and the unexplained.

Haiti is a land steeped in spirituality, where the veil between the living and the dead is thin, almost nonexistent. It is a place where the dead truly walk among the living, and where the supernatural feels as close as the breath you take. In this mystic atmosphere, I experienced astral journeys during sleep, moments that blurred the lines between dreams and waking life. These experiences left an indelible mark on me, shaping my understanding of the world and guiding me towards the story that would become Money, Love and Power.

Additionally, I set pen to paper with another purpose: to honor the love and strength of the women who have shaped my life. This book is a tribute to my biological mother, whose unwavering love has been a constant source of strength, to my late sister, whose resilience has inspired me in ways words can scarcely convey, and to the countless other women whose courage, wisdom, and compassion have left an indelible mark on my soul. Their stories, woven into the fabric of my own, are the true heartbeat of this work.

Accordingly, my mother and sister were the first women in my life. I only knew them for a short while—I was just eight years old when they both passed away. Yet, they left an indelible mark on me. I've come to realize that every woman I've encountered in some way reminds me of them. Every meaningful connection I've had—whether platonic, mentorship, friendship, or romantic—feels linked to the memory of these two women. Even though this story, Money, Love and Power, is a fantastical and mystical fiction, many parts of it are inspired by them.

Furthermore, there have been countless other women who have guided and supported me unconditionally. I'd like to take this opportunity to honor them, and eternize their names into this narrative, as each name resonates in my heart like the beat of an African drum : To name just a few: Tante Jeanette, Madame Thelus (late), Marie Saint-Preux(late), Jocelyne Mayas, Madame Florence Bonhomme-Comeau, Yanick Prophete (late), Dolores En Couleur, Gisele Josme, Maguie Goldstein, Chunyee Miot, Francia Cherry, Shawnta Walcott, Dalida Jeune, Maggie Bellabe, Magalie Theodore, Geralda Jovin and most importantly, the woman who chose me as her son—Madame Lise Marc (late). Each of these women has shared a unique and incredible relationship with me, but "Mommy Lise" was closest to my heart. She was closer to me than even my biological mother. She taught me patience, acceptance, humility, love, responsibility, and endurance. She is the main reason my story, Money, Love and Power, survived. I vividly remember that my biological mother passed away on May 1 and was buried on May 7—Mommy Lise's birthday is on May 7. Because of Mommy Lise's love, I found solace in the loss of my maternal love. Wherever she is now, please pray for her—she was the holiest human being I have ever known, and I cannot stress enough that this book is dedicated to her and her love for Haiti's supreme history and culture.

Another decisive reason, Money, Love and Power is a crucial step toward realizing a movie project I have cherished for over two decades. My aim is to use the love story I created as a foundation to promote Haitian culture and traditions. I am passionate about showcasing the rich heritage and unique traditions of Haiti, and I believe this story can be a powerful way to do that. From the vibrant festivals to the beautiful art, music, Haitian mysticism, syncretism, and cuisine, there's so much to highlight and celebrate.

Lastly, I envision this upcoming film initiative as a vibrant space for collaboration, discussion, and creation, fostering a deeper understanding and appreciation of Haiti's unique cultural narratives. I hope that as you read this, you feel a sense of anticipation and excitement. Enjoy your reading.

Realph Saintil

CHAPTER 1

The Paradox of Loyalty

In the heart of a super-luxurious enclave, where the colors of opulence painted their daily reality, a woman sat in a sleek car alongside Nicky's mom Clara. As they traversed the streets lined with extravagance, their conversation delved into the complexities of romantic entanglements.

"You know," the woman stated with her voice carrying a hint of contemplation, "I dare say that loyalty brings bad luck. Or at least, when you're too faithful, you end up losing."

Clara chuckled, her expression a mixture of curiosity and amusement. "What do you mean by that?"

With a sigh, the woman launched into a tale from her youth. "Let me share this little story with you. In my younger days, I only knew one man—the father of my daughter. When he courted me, his words were like honey, soothing and reassuring. He convinced me to leave my studies, while transitioning from high school to college, just to be with him. He was my first in every sense of the word."

"Yes, I'm not exactly a stranger to the concept," Clara interjected with a knowing smile.

"I loved him so much," the woman continued, her voice tinged with nostalgia, "that when he left the country for twenty years—my daughter's entire lifetime—I remained faithful. But when he returned, he fell under the spell of another girl, who eventually became his wife. Now, here I am, left to navigate the tumult of my own biological clock, resorting to tranquilizers to ease the pain of my shattered dreams. I suppose you could say I'm simply a victim of love and loyalty."

Clara arched an eyebrow, a hint of skepticism in her gaze. "But did you truly have to be a victim? Our lives are simply a reflection of the choices we make, was it not a choice you made to remain loyal to him?"

The woman pondered on this question as their car pulled up to a modern clinic. Clara clutched a prescription and a stack of papers detailing her major health concern—a problem she had come to discuss with her doctor. She was also meeting her husband, Robert, who had separate transportation from work. The conversation lingered in the air, the paradox of loyalty echoing in their minds as they stepped out of the car and into the uncertain realm of a medical consultation.

The woman's story, though brief, resonated in Clara's mind as she walked into the pristine clinic. She couldn't shake off the feeling that loyalty, that steadfast commitment to one person or one ideal, could sometimes lead to heartache and disappointment. Yet wasn't loyalty supposed to be a virtue, a noble quality that bound people together in trust and devotion?

She settled into the chair in the waiting room, but Nicky's mom found herself pondering the nature of loyalty. Was it truly a double-edged sword, capable of both protecting and betraying those who held it dear? Or was there a way to navigate the treacherous waters of fidelity without sacrificing one's own happiness and well-being?

As the familiar scent of antiseptic permeated the air, patients bustled about the waiting room of Dr.

Thompson's clinic. Among them was Clara leaning on her crutch for support, her husband Robert's protective hands guiding her through the crowd. Their faces etched with concern, embarking on their journey towards healing.

"Hi ma'am, can I help you?" The receptionist's voice cut through the hustle and bustle, addressing Clara.

Robert, a regular visitor to the clinic, approached the secretary's desk with a sense of purpose and handed over the prescriptions. After conversing with the clinical assistant at the front desk, Clara's thoughts drifted back to the woman's tale, to the sacrifices she had made in the name of love and loyalty. Had she been too trusting, too willing to overlook the signs of her partner's betrayal? Or had she simply been unlucky, a victim of circumstances beyond her control?

The physician's assistant called out her name, she rose to her feet, her mind still swirling with questions and doubts. The door to the consultation room opened and as she followed the doctor inside, she couldn't help but wonder if loyalty was truly a paradox—a puzzle with no easy solution, no clear path forward.

Inside, Dr. Thompson greeted Clara and Robert with a warm smile, their familiarity evident in their exchanged glances. Their relationship extended beyond the professional realm, hinting at a shared history. As they engaged in conversation, their lingered an unspoken understanding represented a silent acknowledgment of past encounters.

With a gentle demeanor, Dr. Thompson proceeded to examine Clara offering medical advice with care and precision. Each word uttered carried the weight of experience, a testament to the trust forged between patient and physician. Throughout the consultation, as the doctor explained her condition and outlined possible treatment options, Clara found herself grappling with conflicting emotions. On the one hand, she wanted to trust the doctor, to believe that he had her best interests at heart. On the other hand, she couldn't shake off the feeling of unease, the nagging doubt that loyalty could sometimes blind people to the truth.

As the consultation ended, Robert and Clara bid farewell to the doctor, gratitude etched in their expression.

Exiting the consultation room, they and Dr. Thompson parted ways, their paths diverging once more. Yet, the bond forged within the confines of the clinic endured, a testament to the enduring connection between healer and healed.

As she left the clinic, new prescription in hand, Clara couldn't help but feel a sense of relief mingled with apprehension. She knew that the road ahead would be difficult, fraught with challenges and uncertainties, but she also knew that she couldn't afford to let loyalty, even to her doctor, cloud her judgment to blindly follow a path that might lead to further heartache and disappointment.

And so, as she returned to the sleek car waiting outside, Clara made a silent vow to herself. She would remain loyal to those she loved, to those who had earned her trust and devotion. But she would also remain vigilant, always mindful of the potential pitfalls of blind faith and unwavering loyalty.

While the car pulled away from the curb and merged into the bustling city streets, Clara felt a sense of determination stirring within her. She knew that the paradox of loyalty would continue to intrigue her, to test her resolve and challenge her beliefs. But she also knew that she was strong enough to face whatever obstacles lay ahead, armed with the wisdom gained from her own experiences and the stories of those who had come before her.

With her head held high and her heart filled with hope, she embarked on the next chapter of her journey—a journey marked by the timeless struggle to reconcile the conflicting demands of loyalty and self-preservation, to find a balance between devotion and independence, between love and loss.

As the days turned into weeks and the weeks turned into months, Clara found herself confronting the paradox of loyalty in a myriad of ways. From her relationships with family and friends to her own sense of self-worth and identity, she grappled with the age-old question of how to remain true to oneself without sacrificing one's loyalty to others.

Through it all, she remained steadfast in her resolve, refusing to let the paradox of loyalty define her or dictate her choices. For she knew that true loyalty was not about blindly following others or sacrificing one's own happiness for the sake of others. It was about finding a balance, a middle ground where one could remain true to oneself while also honoring the bonds of love and devotion that connected them to others.

As she navigated the twists and turns of life's journey, she embraced the paradox of loyalty as a challenge to be faced rather than a burden to be borne. For she knew that it was only by confronting the contradictions within herself and within the world around her that she could truly discover the depth of her own strength and resilience.

The years passed and the world continued to change around her. Nicky's mom remained true to herself and to those she loved. She knew that in the end, it was not blind loyalty or unwavering devotion that defined her, but rather the courage to confront the paradox of loyalty with an open heart and a steadfast resolve.

And in that courage, she found her truest self—the self that was neither bound by the expectations of others nor constrained by the limitations of her own fears and doubts.

As she looked back on her life and all the challenges she had faced, Clara smiled knowing that she had lived with courage and integrity, embracing the paradox of loyalty as a testament to the strength of her own character and the depth of her own humanity.

CHAPTER 2

CLARA'S Dilemma:
A Journey of Faith and
Friendship

As Clara left her doctor's office, her mind swirled with a multitude of emotions. The weight of the news from the results of her consultation and various analyses sat heavy upon her shoulders. With a heavy heart, she made her way to her friend's house, seeking solace and counsel in the comforting presence of someone she trusted.

Upon arriving, she found her friend and another woman engrossed in conversation, their voices hushed in the intimacy of shared confidences. Eager to unburden herself, she joined them, her thoughts already consumed by the proposal her husband had recently put forth.

The conversation took a sharp turn as her friend's friend voiced her opinion on the matter. "It seems that you have received quite the proposition," she remarked, her tone laden with implications. "To accept such a thing... it's unthinkable."

Her friend chimed in, her words cutting through the air like a knife. "Imagine being in the shoes of the woman who would receive a million dollars to bear a child for a couple, especially if she's not already entangled with the husband," she said, her words dripping with bitterness. "To allow your husband to sleep with another, to carry and nurture a child that will never truly be yours... it's a betrayal beyond comprehension."

The weight of their words pressed down on Clara, suffocating her with their harsh truths. "You would lose all semblance of authority over your husband," the woman continued, her voice filled with sympathy. "And that child, no matter how much you may love and care for it, will never see you as its true mother. It's a burden you should not bear willingly."

Yet amidst the darkness, a glimmer of hope emerged as her friend offered words of solace and guidance. "There is still hope for you," she said, with a soft yet firm voice. "Turn to your faith, seek solace in prayer and devotion. Let the love of God and the Blessed Virgin Mary be your guiding light in this time of darkness."

Her friend's words struck a chord within the woman's heart, stirring a newfound resolve within her soul. With renewed determination, she vowed to seek refuge in her faith, to find strength in the love of her family and friends.

And so, the woman's path forward became clear. Armed with faith and fortified by the bonds of friendship, she faced the uncertain future with courage and grace, ready to confront whatever challenges lay ahead.

CHAPTER 3

A Conversation at the Crossroads

As the sun dipped below the horizon, casting long shadows across the city streets, Robert stepped out of his office building, his mind preoccupied with the events of the day. With a weary sigh, he made his way to his car, eager to return home and unwind after a long day's work.

Fate had other plans for Robert that evening as he found himself pulling into a gas station to refuel his car. It was there, amidst the faint scent of gasoline and the hum of distant traffic, that he encountered an old friend.

"Julian!" Robert exclaimed, a smile spreading across his face as he spotted the familiar figure approaching him. The two men embraced warmly, exchanging pleasantries and catching up on each other's lives.

"How are you, old friend?" Julian inquired, his eyes twinkling with mischief. "Still the same incorrigible womanizer I remember?"

Robert chuckled, shaking his head. "You flatter me, Julian. But no, I've changed my ways since getting married."

The mention of marriage seemed to sober Julian's expression, and he regarded Robert with a thoughtful gaze. "Speaking of marriage, how's your wife? Any children yet?"

Robert's smile faltered slightly at the mention of children, and he sighed heavily. "No, Julian. It seems we won't be having any children of our own."

Julian's eyebrows shot up in surprise. "I'm sorry to hear that, Robert. Have you sought medical advice?"

Robert nodded; his expression pained. "We've been to countless doctors, tried every treatment imaginable. But it seems my wife is unable to conceive."

Julian placed a sympathetic hand on Robert's shoulder. "I can't imagine how difficult this must be for you both.

But remember, there's more to life than just children. You and your wife can still find happiness together."

Robert managed a weak smile, grateful for Julian's words of encouragement. "Thank you, Julian. Your support means a lot to me."

As the conversation ended, the two friends exchanged a firm handshake and a shared understanding. Though life had thrown them a curveball, they knew they would face it together, with strength and resilience.

And as Robert drove away into the night, he couldn't help but feel a glimmer of hope amidst the uncertainty. For in the face of adversity, true friendship was the beacon that guided him home.

CHAPTER 4

The Gilded Cage

As the evening sun dipped below the horizon, casting a warm glow over the sprawling mansion, Clara returned home. The imposing gates swung open to welcome her into the realm of opulence she inhabited with her husband, Robert. The house stood as a testament to their success, its grandeur overshadowed only by the weight of their unspoken desires.

In the foyer, Robert, clad in his pajamas, greeted her with a tender kiss and a tight embrace. Their footsteps echoed through the marble halls as they made their way to the dining room, a scene of lavish abundance that bespoke their affluent lifestyle.

Amidst the extravagance, Clara's appetite waned. She pushed her food around her plate, the taste of opulence bitter on her tongue. Excusing herself, she retreated to the solitude of her chamber, a sanctuary adorned with treasures of a different kind.

In the dim light, Clara lovingly caressed a collection of dolls, their delicate features frozen in perpetual innocence. Each one held a piece of her heart, a silent reminder of the children she yearned for but could never have. Tears welled in her eyes, silent witnesses to the ache in her soul.

Robert found her there, his presence a mixture of comfort and constraint. With practiced ease, he delivered the news of his triumphs, his words a symphony of success that reverberated hollow in Clara's ears. She listened but with her heart heavy by the weight of unspoken dreams.

"We will do adoptions for the legacy of it all," she whispered, her voice a fragile thread of hope amidst the tapestry of their reality.

Robert's gaze softened, understanding dawning in his eyes. He closed his laptop, the glow of the screen fading into oblivion as he reached for her hand. In that moment, beneath the facade of wealth and power, they were simply two souls bound by love and longing.

As the night stretched on, their whispered conversations filled the air, weaving a tapestry of dreams and aspirations. And though the path ahead was uncertain, they walked it together, their hearts united in the pursuit of a legacy that transcended wealth and privilege.

In the gilded cage of their existence, Clara and Robert found solace in each other, their love a beacon of light amidst the shadows of their unspoken desires. And as they faced the future hand in hand, they knew that together, they could weather any storm that came their way.

CHAPTER 5

The DREAMING lady

In the vivid landscape of her dream, Clara finds herself amidst a sea of hundreds of children, their cries echoing around her like a haunting melody. Surrounding them are statues of undressed kids, each one a symbol of innocence and vulnerability. Among them, she notices four distinct figures – twin girls and two little boys – their nakedness suggesting a purity untouched by the constraints of society.

Candles flicker ominously, their light extinguished one by one, accompanied by a chilling musical suspense that sends shivers down her spine. Suddenly, four babies appear, chasing after her with urgency, their innocent faces a stark contrast to the foreboding atmosphere.

In a heart-stopping moment, she teeters on the edge of a cliff, the abyss yawning beneath her threatening to swallow her whole. With a jolt, she awakens, her heart racing, her mind grappling with the cryptic messages hidden within the dream. For her, the abrupt awakening signifies impending complexity, while the cries of the children speak of profound sadness lurking just beneath the surface.

The sight of undressed children brings a glimmer of hope, a promise of unexpected joy waiting to be discovered. Yet, the dwindling candles cast a shadow of impending doom, a reminder of ongoing hardships yet to be faced. The specter of falling off a cliff serves as a stark warning, a call to tread carefully lest she succumb to the pitfalls of misfortune.

In this surreal tapestry of dreams and symbols, Clara is left to decipher the tangled web of her subconscious, seeking meaning amidst the chaos of her psyche.

CHAPTER 6

The COURTROOM

In the courtroom, amidst the solemnity of legal proceedings, a poignant saga unfolds. Clara and Robert stand facing a woman who entrusted them with her precious little girl for adoption. What began as an act of trust and hope now stands as a contentious debate, meticulously prepared for this very moment. As the judge prepares to render a decision, the weight of emotions hangs heavy in the air.

Clara and Robert, once filled with anticipation and joy at the prospect of expanding their family, now find themselves entangled in a legal battle fraught with emotional complexities. The woman who placed her child in their care watches intently, her own heart undoubtedly torn between love and the legal obligations she faces.

Legal arguments are presented with precision and clarity. Lawyers articulate the rights and responsibilities of each party involved, navigating through intricate statutes and precedents. The judge listens attentively, weighing the evidence before rendering a decision that will shape the lives of everyone present.

After careful consideration of the facts and legal arguments presented, the judge delivers a verdict. In a moment that reverberates through the courtroom, the girl is returned to her biological mother. The courtroom erupts with a mixture of relief, disbelief, and heartache. For Clara, the decision strikes a devastating blow, leaving her shattered and inconsolable.

As the courtroom empties, the echoes of the day's events linger in the hearts and minds of all involved. Clara returns home, her spirit broken, her grief overwhelming. In the solitude of her own anguish, she grapples with the agony of losing a child she had come to love as her own. The bond she shared with her remains unbroken, a testament to the enduring power of love in the face of adversity.

This case served as a poignant reminder of the complexities inherent in matters of adoption and parental rights. Beyond the legal intricacies lies a realm of profound emotion, where love and loss intertwine in a delicate dance. As Clara seeks solace in the memories she holds dear, her journey serves as a testament to the resilience of the human spirit in the face of life's most formidable challenges.

Soon after this devastating decision, Clara and Robert decided to embark on a short vacation to release from the emotional roller coaster they had experienced.

As the cruise ship gently glided through the azure waters, Robert was steadfast in his commitment to pleasing his wife, even when faced with difficulties. Amidst dinners illuminated by the soft glow of candlelight and impressive surprise outings filled with vibrant colors, the allure of parenthood lingered persistently.

Amid such apparent joys, the tempting choice of having their own child remained a constant presence. Despite the stress that occasionally crept in, bicycle outings served to chase away any lingering anxieties.

Clara unfolded in a moment reminiscent of the advice from her friend, reminding her that all hope was not lost. As she gazed out over the tranquil expanse of the ocean, a sense of possibility mingled with uncertainty in her heart.

The gentle sway of the ship mirrored the ebb and flow of emotions within them as they navigated the complexities of their desires and aspirations. Each passing moment brought them closer to a decision that would shape their lives irrevocably.

Amidst the backdrop of the vast ocean and starlit skies, Nicky's parents found themselves at a crossroads, torn between the comfort of their current existence and the tantalizing prospect of expanding their family.

As they retired to their cabin for the night, the gentle lullaby of the waves served as a soothing reminder of the journey that lay ahead. The allure of parenthood beckoned to them, promising both joy and challenges in equal measure.

With each passing day, they found themselves drawn inexorably towards the realization of their deepest desires. And amidst the uncertainty of the future, they discovered a newfound sense of purpose and resolve.

In the quiet moments of reflection, they found solace in the knowledge that whatever path they chose, they would embark upon it together, united in love and determination.

And as the cruise ship continued its journey through the vast expanse of the ocean, Nicky's parents embraced the uncertainty of the future, knowing that whatever lay ahead, they would face it with courage and conviction.

The temptation of parenthood remained ever-present, a beacon of hope amidst the tumultuous seas of life. And as they looked towards the horizon, Nicky's parents knew that their greatest adventure was yet to come.

CHAPTER 7

The Sacred Gathering

As the sun dipped below the horizon, casting hues of orange and pink across the sky, the small-town square came to life with an otherworldly energy. The church bell tolled, its sound reverberating through the air like the harmonious voices of angels. Accompanied by the distant beat of a drum, it set the stage for what was to come.

A group of men and women, all dressed in pristine white garments, gathered in front of the ancient church. Their heads were decorated with various adornments — some with whalebone headpieces, others with flickering candles, and still more with delicate white flowers. Each accessory held its own significance, a symbol of devotion and reverence.

Amidst the gathering, one figure stood out – Nicky's mother. She approached the church with purpose, her eyes alight with determination. At the foot of the church facade, she knelt before a makeshift altar, decked with offerings of flowers and candles. This was the moment she had been waiting for, the culmination of her deepest desires.

Meanwhile, unbeknownst to the human eye, silent observers stood guard. Sane statues, indistinguishable from their inert counterparts, concealed a secret purpose. Behind each figure lay a hidden notebook, its pages waiting to record the wishes and grievances of those who sought solace in this sacred space.

Among the cacophony of whispered prayers and fervent pleas, the voices of the seekers rang out:

"I came to seek wealth," one proclaimed, his voice tinged with desperation.

"I came for a woman I love. I will reward you with anything if you send me to have her," another implored, his words a testament to his unyielding devotion.

And then there was Nicky's mother, her words a poignant declaration of her heart's deepest desire. "I want to have a child at any price," she confessed, her voice trembling with emotion.

As the night wore on, the air grew thick with anticipation. Each supplicant poured their heart out to the unseen guardians, their hopes and fears laid bare before the divine. And amidst the flickering candlelight and the solemn silence of the statues, the sacred gathering continued, a testament to the enduring power of faith and devotion.

CHAPTER 8

The Night of Revelation

As she entered her home, the weight of the revelation she carried seemed to deepen with each step. Her heart raced, anticipation mingling with apprehension as she approached her husband. Tonight was unlike any other; tonight, she bore a burden too heavy to share.

With trembling lips, she uttered the words that would forever alter the course of their lives. Her husband, whose touch once brought comfort and solace, now stood before her, a mere spectator to the unraveling of their reality. "I will sleep alone tonight," she declared, her voice barely above a whisper, as if afraid to give voice to the ominous prophecy that had befallen her.

In their room, a sanctuary of intimacy and love, she prepared for a night of solitude. The ambiance, seemingly plucked from the pages of a fairytale, did little to assuage the weight of her premonition. Candles flickered, casting dancing shadows upon the walls, while pristine white sheets adorned the bed, each corner a cardinal point in the tableau of her fate.

She bathed herself in perfume, anointing her skin with fragrant oils in a futile attempt to cleanse herself of the foreboding that clung to her like a shroud. Braids of linen intertwined with her fingers, a futile attempt to tether herself to the reality she once knew.

As sleep enveloped her, she descended into a dreamscape fraught with symbolism and portent. A baby, falling from a cross, its tiny form a stark echo of a familiar narrative. Instinctively, she reached out, cradling the child in her arms, a savior in the darkness of her subconscious.

Yet, as quickly as the vision had come, it was shattered by the harsh light of reality. Smoke filled the room, an ethereal haze obscuring her surroundings. From its midst emerged a figure, cloaked in white, a harbinger of the fateful bargain that awaited her. "You will catch him," the figure intoned, its voice a symphony of promises and threats. "But your husband will be no more."

With each word, the weight of her decision bore down upon her, a burden too heavy for mortal shoulders to bear. And yet, in the depths of her soul, she knew what she must do.

"Agree to this, and your son shall thrive," the figure continued, its voice a siren's call laced with temptation. "He shall marry my daughter, and together they shall forge a new legacy."

In a world where boundaries blurred and taboos were but whispers in the wind, the choice before her was clear. Sacrifice one love for the promise of another, forsake the familiar for the allure of the unknown.

And so, with a heavy heart and a silent prayer upon her lips, she gave her answer. A nod, a whisper, a silent acquiescence to the destiny that awaited her. The saint then took on a human appearance and grabbed Clara, undressed her and put her to bed in an inhumane way and immediately after she saw herself and the saint transform into a stool statue, the figure disappeared and she for her part covered his human body. As the figure vanished into the night, she knew that her path was set, her fate irrevocably sealed.

As she witnesses the miraculous transformation of herself and the saint into a stool statue, a profound sense of wonder envelops her. In the wake of this surreal moment, the saint vanishes into the unknown, leaving her to grapple with the inexplicable occurrence. Despite the figure's disappearance, she instinctively moves to protect his human form, a gesture born from a deep sense of reverence and duty. Standing amidst the enigmatic aftermath, she finds solace in the profound connection forged through this extraordinary experience. In this moment of uncertainty and awe, she realizes the enduring power of faith and the profound impact of divine intervention.

Alone in the darkness, she surrendered to the embrace of sleep, knowing that when she awoke, her world would be forever changed.

CHAPTER 9

A Father's farewell Journey

Robert leaned in to kiss his wife goodbye, his lips lingering for a moment before he straightened up, his expression a mixture of affection and determination. The morning sun cast a warm glow as he grabbed his car keys and headed out the door, his mind already occupied with the day ahead.

As he stepped outside, the familiar strains of a song filled the air, emanating from a passing car. The lyrics resonated with him, speaking of love and acceptance in the face of reality's challenges. He paused for a moment, allowing the music to wash over him, before shaking his head and continuing towards his car.

The music faded into the distance behind him as his car engine roared to life. He pulled out of the driveway with thoughts of his plans for the day, the tasks and meetings that awaited him. Without warning, tragedy struck. Time seemed to slow as another vehicle collided with his sending shards of glass flying. The screech of tires, the sickening crunch of metal against metal.

In an instant, everything changed. The air was thick with the smell of burning rubber and gasoline as Robert found himself trapped in the wreckage, pain searing through his body. For all his wealth and success, for all the comforts that money could buy, it had done nothing to shield him from this moment. In the end, it was not wealth or possessions that mattered, but the love and connections he had forged along the way. And so, as the darkness closed in around him, Robert whispered a silent prayer of gratitude for the life he had lived, for the love he had known.

As he lay there, his life slipping away, he understood that true happiness could not be bought or sold, it was found in the simple moments, in the laughter of loved ones and the warmth of human connection. For in the end, that was all that truly mattered.

The first condition of Clara's revelation had been met, cruel and unforgiving. Death had come knocking, a stark reminder of life's fragility. And in its wake, a profound realization began to dawn.

As the somber skies wept, a congregation gathered, a sea of mourners huddled beneath the weight of grief. Families intertwined, friends leaned on each other for support, their faces etched with sorrow. The priest's words, simple yet profound, hung heavy in the air, offering solace to the shattered hearts.

A procession of cars wound its solemn path through the streets, each vehicle a vessel of memories, carrying loved ones to the final farewell. The cemetery beckoned, its silent expanse a sanctuary for the departed. Innocent flowers adorned the graves, their delicate petals a poignant contrast to the harsh reality of loss.

Amidst the sea of mourners, stood a woman, her sorrow palpable, her tears a testament to the pain that gripped her soul. Yet, amidst the sorrow, a subtle miracle unfolded – she was already pregnant, a beacon of hope amidst the darkness. Despite the outpouring of condolences, she remained inconsolable, her heart shattered by the weight of her grief.

As the final words of the priest's prayer faded into the distance, the mourners dispersed, leaving behind the echoes of their sorrow. Life and death danced in an eternal embrace, a poignant reminder of the vulnerability of existence.

The somber notes of grief lingered in the air as loved ones gathered in the familiar embrace of home, seeking solace after bidding farewell to a cherished soul. Memories danced like shadows across the walls, echoing laughter mingled with tears, as stories of shared moments weaved a tapestry of remembrance and longing. During sorrow's embrace, a twist of fate whispers hope, as the joyous news of new life emerges, casting a shimmering light upon the gathering's darkness. Hearts heavy with loss find unexpected buoyancy, as the promise of tomorrow blooms within the tender embrace of a newborn's first cry.

In the midst of tears of sorrow and tears of joy, the melody of life continues its refrain, harmonizing the bitter and the sweet, weaving a symphony of love that transcends the bounds of time and space.

CHAPTER 10

The Arrival of the Albino

In the bustling emergency room, the air is charged with anticipation. Doctors and nurses move with purpose, their determination palpable as they prepare for the final stages of labor. Clara lies on the delivery bed, her body tense with the exertion of childbirth.

Amidst the controlled chaos, there is a sense of wonder and curiosity surrounding this birth. The child that is about to enter the world carries with it a rare and unexpected trait - albinism. Whispers of speculation fill the room, alluding to the uniqueness of the newborn's appearance and the mysteries that shroud it.

As the woman's contractions intensify, the medical team springs into action, their expertise guiding them through the delicate process. With each passing moment, the anticipation mounts until finally, with a cry that pierces the air, Nicky is born.

Silence descends upon the room as all eyes turn to the tiny bundle cradled in the doctor's arms. The infant's pallid skin and ethereal features stand out in stark contrast to the bustling activity around them, marking them as something truly extraordinary. For a moment, the world seems to hold its breath, captivated by the sight before them. And then, as if on cue, the room erupts into a chorus of awe and wonder, celebrating the arrival of this unique and precious life.

As the medical team tends to the newborn and his mother, the significance of this moment is not lost on them, for in the birth of this albino child, they are reminded of the miracle of life itself, and the boundless possibilities that lie within every one of us.

Amidst the joy and excitement, there lingers a sense of solemnity, a recognition of the challenges that lie ahead for this child born different from the rest. And yet, there is also hope for a future where diversity is embraced and celebrated, where differences are seen not as limitations, but as sources of strength and beauty.

CHAPTER 11

The Baptism and Surreal underground gathering of albino individuals

As the church bells chimed, Nicky's mom, filled with anticipation, entered the sacred space adorned with candles flickering in the dim light. Nicky, nestled in his mother's arms, gazed around in wonder unaware of the significance of the moment about to unfold. At the altar, the priest draped in ceremonial robes, prepared the holy water for the baptism. As he recited the sacred words, a hush fell over the congregation. As the water touched Nicky's forehead, a cry pierced the air like a lament from the depths of the soul.

To the shock of all present, the container holding the holy water began emitting vapors, swirling, and dancing in the air. As the priest made the sign of the cross with the holy water over the other children awaiting baptism, a profound transformation occurred. The clear liquid turned crimson, resembling the very blood that flowed from the wounds of Christ on the cross.

Meanwhile, in a hidden chamber beneath the earth, a grand reception was underway. Albino figures, cloaked in scarlet robes, moved gracefully among tables decorated with thousands of red bottles and a magnificent white cake. In their midst lay Nicky, swaddled in white, a symbol of innocence amidst the crimson-clad throng.

As the rain poured down outside, Nicky's albino father stepped forward, his voice carrying the weight of centuries. "My son," he declared, "when you walk among the earthlings, you shall be a messenger of our kind. They, small in spirit, shall come to know us, the neutral angels who dwell in the depths below."

With reverence, he continued, "We are the descendants of the twelve apostles, cast out by God yet endowed with great power. It is we who reside underground, in communion with humanity, our pure waters reflecting the very image of paradise."

The moon's reflection shimmered upon a tranquil pool, mirroring the beauty of the flowers that adorned its banks. Yet, juxtaposed against this serene backdrop was the reality of the albino realm, where power and mystery intertwined in the depths below.

Amidst whispers of ancient prophecy, Nicky's mother, a vision of Saint Anne herself, spoke with fervent devotion. "You shall grow", she proclaimed, "in the likeness of your brothers, giants in stature and radiance. For you, my child, are destined for greatness."

With solemn reverence, the baby was placed in a cradle as white as snow, the smoke of burning incense rising to meet the heavens. And as the ethereal mist drifted upwards, a connection was forged between the earthly realm and the unseen forces that guided Nicky's destiny.

CHAPTER 12

Nicky's Arrival in Madrid: A Reunion of Familiar Faces

2 5 Years later, as the plane touched down on the runway of Madrid's bustling airport, Nicky's heart raced with anticipation. He glanced out of the window, eager to catch a glimpse of the city he had heard so much about. As the passengers began to gather their belongings and shuffle towards the exit, Nicky felt a surge of excitement mixed with a hint of nervousness. This was it – the beginning of his adventure in Spain. Stepping off the plane, Nicky was greeted by the chatter

of passengers, the hum of machinery, the occasional announcement over the loudspeaker.

Amidst the chaos, one voice stood out – a warm, familiar tone calling his name. Turning towards the sound, Nicky spotted a familiar face in the crowd. A lady with kind eyes and a warm smile. It was his mother's friend; someone he hadn't seen in years.

"Look, it's unbelievable," the lady exclaimed, her eyes widening in surprise as she took in Nicky's appearance. "A big, well-built boy, so you pass the milestone of 50 girls, huh! Come explain to your second mother." Nicky couldn't help but chuckle at her words. It felt good to be welcomed with such warmth and humor, even after all this time.

With a smile, Nicky made his way over to the lady, embracing her in a warm hug. "It's good to see you," his voice filled with genuine affection. "I've missed you." The lady returned the hug, holding Nicky close for a moment before pulling back to look at him with a fond smile.

As they caught up on old times, Nicky couldn't help but feel a sense of gratitude for the people in his life – the ones who had supported him, encouraged him, and welcomed him with open arms. It was moments like these that reminded him of the importance of friendship, of connection, of the bonds that held us together, no matter how far apart we may be.

But as much as he cherished the reunion with his mother's friend, Nicky knew that there were others waiting for him – friends who had come to pick him up and whisk him away to new adventures in this vibrant city.

With a reluctant smile, Nicky excused himself from the conversation, promising to catch up with the lady later. Now, heading towards the exit, he scanned the crowd, searching for familiar faces among the throngs of people. Then, he spotted them – a group of friends standing near the entrance, waving excitedly and calling out his name. With a grin, he quickened his pace, eager to join them and begin this new chapter of his journey. As he approached the group, Nicky was greeted with cheers and hugs, laughter and excitement. It felt good to be surrounded by friends, to know that he was not alone in this foreign land. Together, they made their way towards the waiting car, chatting and laughing as they recounted memories and made plans for the days ahead.

As they drove through the streets of Madrid, Nicky felt a sense of exhilaration – the thrill of being in a new place, of experiencing new sights and sounds, of embarking on a new adventure. And as he looked out of the window at the passing scenery, he knew that this was only the beginning – the start of something beautiful and exciting.

With a smile, Nicky leaned back in his seat, feeling grateful for the journey that had brought him here, for the friends who had welcomed him with open arms, for the opportunities that lay ahead. As the car made its way through the bustling streets of Madrid, Nicky closed his eyes and let himself be swept away by the excitement and promise of the unknown.

CHAPTER 13

The Botanical Park

In the serene beauty of the botanical park, Nicky and Marytza's paths converged, igniting a dreamlike encounter. Amidst the fragrant blooms and winding pathways, their meeting unfolded like a scene from a romantic novel. Nicky's gaze fell upon Marytza, a vision of ethereal beauty in the thick of the verdant landscape. Summoning his courage, he approached her, his heart racing with anticipation.

Initiating the conversation, Nicky expressed his admiration for Marytza's allure, confessing his initial hesitations in approaching her. Marytza, in turn, countered his perception of innocence with a poignant reflection on the complexities of human nature.

During their exchange, Nicky and Marytza discovered a shared affinity for intellect and wit. Their banter revealed a mutual appreciation for meaningful communication, laying the foundation for a deeper connection.

In a candid moment, Nicky revealed his criteria for love, emphasizing attraction, communication, shared goals, and intimate compatibility. Marytza, intrigued by his honesty, reciprocated by expressing her own desires, symbolized by a bouquet of white flowers.

Despite their differences, Nicky and Marytza found solace in laughter, bridging the gap between their worlds with humor and mutual respect. Their playful exchange underscored the depth of their connection, transcending societal norms and expectations.

As their conversation deepened, Nicky and Marytza peeled back the layers of their identities, revealing vulnerabilities and insecurities. In each other's presence, they found solace and acceptance, forging a bond rooted in authenticity.

Navigating the complexities of love and desire, Nicky and Marytza embraced the nuances of their relationship, acknowledging the intricacies of human connection. In their shared journey, they discovered beauty in imperfection and strength in vulnerability.

As the dream ended, Nicky and Marytza leaned in for a kiss, their lips meeting in a tender embrace. Though their time together was fleeting, the memory of their encounter lingered, a testament to the enduring power of love and connection. Enveloped in the dream's enchanting embrace, Nicky and Marytza were abruptly jolted awake, returning to their separate realities. Their fleeting moment of intimacy evaporated like morning mist, leaving them yearning for more.

CHAPTER 14

Nicky's experience: homecoming

As Nicky stepped through the front door of his mother's house, he was greeted with the familiar scent of home. His mother, standing in the hallway, rushed to embrace him, her eyes shining with love. "Welcome home, my dear," she said, her voice filled with warmth.

Clara enveloped him in a tight hug, planting a kiss on his cheek. She looked at him with eyes full of affection, seeing him not just as her son, but as her pride and joy. "You're my only jewel," she whispered, her words carrying the weight of a mother's unconditional love.

Returning home always filled Nicky with a sense of comfort and belonging. No matter where life took him, his mother's house remained his sanctuary, a place where he could find solace and love amidst the chaos of the world.

After exchanging pleasantries with his mother, Nicky made his way to his room, a familiar path he had walked countless times before. It was a ritual of sorts, one that brought him a sense of peace and familiarity in the midst of life's uncertainties.

Alone in his room, Nicky took a moment to reflect on his journey. The walls adorned with memories of his past, each photograph and trinket holding a special place in his heart. It was in this quiet solitude that he found clarity and perspective, allowing him to make sense of the world around him.

From the window of his room, Nicky watched the world go by. The hustle and bustle of everyday life seemed to fade away as he gazed out at the serene landscape before him. In that moment, he felt a sense of gratitude for the simple joys of home and family.

As Nicky sat on his bed, memories of his childhood came flooding back. He remembered playing in the backyard with his friends, the laughter echoing through the air. His mother's voice calling him in for dinner, the smell of her cooking wafting through the house. These were the moments that shaped him, the foundation upon which his life was built.

Thinking of his mother, Nicky couldn't help but feel a profound sense of gratitude. She had sacrificed so much for him, always putting his needs above her own. Her love was a constant presence in his life, guiding him through the ups and downs with unwavering support.

As the evening sun dipped below the horizon, Nicky felt a sense of contentment wash over him. These moments, spent in the comfort of his mother's home, were ones he cherished above all else. It was here, surrounded by love and warmth, that he truly felt at peace.

As the night ended, Nicky knew that this homecoming would be one to remember. In the embrace of his mother's love, he found strength and reassurance for the journey ahead. For no matter where life took him, he knew that he would always have a place to call home.

CHAPTER 15

Nicky's Vision

Nicky sat in a moment of contemplation, allowing his mind to wander into a realm where imagination took flight. In this ethereal landscape, a symphony of imagery unfolded before his eyes.

In a sea of white, Nicky found himself surrounded by countless feline companions, their soft fur brushing against his feet as they curled up in peaceful slumber. As he watched, delicate white butterflies emerged, gracefully ascending towards the heavens, their wings shimmering in the sunlight.

Next, his gaze was drawn to a pair of pigeons, their tender embrace is a testament to love's enduring power.

Their affectionate kisses painted a picture of harmony and unity, filling Nicky's heart with warmth.

Yet, amidst this idyllic scene, a figure caught Nicky's attention—an albino young lady, her presence both enigmatic and mesmerizing. She moved with grace and elegance, her every step a testament to the beauty of the human form. Clad in the attire of an opera dancer, she embodied the very essence of purity and innocence.

As Nicky continued to observe, he became aware of a voice, resonating with the timbre of his father's, weaving a tapestry of words that danced upon the air. It was as if the voice itself were reciting poetry, each word imbued with meaning and emotion.

"My dear son, allow me to convey a message of profound significance. You see, there exists someone in your life, a beacon of light amidst the darkness, who eagerly awaits your presence. She embodies the very essence of your existence, resonating with the melody of your soul, the rhythm of your heart. She is not merely a fleeting presence, but rather the very fabric of your universe, a symphony of love and devotion.

I implore you to recognize her as the diamond amidst the rough, a precious gem waiting to be uncovered with each passing moment. She is your solace, your sanctuary, akin to the soothing strains of classical music that envelop your being with tranquility and peace.

As you journey through the tapestry of time, she will stand by your side, a steadfast companion through life's trials and triumphs. And even as the years unfurl like delicate petals in the wind, her love will endure, an unwavering flame in the vast expanse of eternity.

Imagine, if you will, a scene where an Albino girl extends her hand, offering white flowers at her feet, beckoning you to join her in a world of infinite possibility. "Take my hand, Nicky," she whispers, "and together, let us vanish into the ether, where our love knows no bounds."

So, my dear son, heed these words and embrace the love that awaits you, for in her embrace lies the truest treasure you will ever know."

Within the cadence of this poetic declamation, the young lady began to disrobe, her movements slow and deliberate. Piece by piece, her garments fell away, until she stood before Nicky, bathed in the soft glow of moonlight. And yet, it was not just her outer attire that was shed, but also the metaphorical barriers that separated them, revealing a deeper connection that transcended the physical realm.

In this moment of revelation, Nicky understood that what lay beneath the surface was far more precious than any material possession. It was a bond forged in the fires of shared experience and mutual understanding, a bond that could never be bought or sold.

And so, as the vision faded and reality began to take hold once more, Nicky carried with him the memory of that fleeting glimpse into the depths of his own soul—a reminder that true beauty lies not in what can be seen with the eyes, but in what can only be felt with the heart.

CHAPTER 16

Marytza's Experience: The Enigma of Marytza's Sleepwalking

In a quaint little house nestled among the trees, Marytza's unusual sleepwalking habits puzzled her family. It was a sight to behold as she wandered around the house with her eyes tightly shut, yet seemingly aware of her surroundings.

Every night, like clockwork, Marytza embarked on her nocturnal journey, walking with purpose through the corridors of her home. Her siblings, curious yet concerned, often found themselves trailing behind her, witnessing the spectacle unfold.

Despite her eyes being closed, Marytza claimed to see everything around her as if guided by an unseen force. Her siblings, eager to understand this strange phenomenon, observed her closely, hoping for a glimpse into her nocturnal world.

While Marytza's sleepwalking seemed harmless at first, her family grew increasingly worried about her well-being. They feared she might inadvertently harm herself or become lost in the labyrinth of her own home.

Desperate for answers, Marytza's family consulted doctors and specialists, hoping to unravel the mystery behind her peculiar behavior. Yet, despite numerous tests and examinations, no concrete explanation could be found.

As they grappled with the enigma of Marytza's sleepwalking, her siblings grew closer, united in their determination to protect and understand her. Together, they formed a tight-knit bond, ready to face whatever challenges lay ahead.

Night after night, Marytza continued her nocturnal wanderings, her siblings by her side, offering comfort and support. They marveled at her ability to navigate the darkness with such ease, as if guided by an unseen hand.

With each passing night, Marytza's family learned to embrace the unknown, accepting her sleepwalking as a part of who she was. They found solace in the fact that, despite the uncertainty, they were always there to watch over her.

In time, Marytza's sleepwalking became less of a mystery and more of a cherished aspect of their family life. They no longer feared the darkness, but instead found comfort in the knowledge that they were together, bound by love and understanding.

As the years passed, Marytza's sleepwalking remained a constant in their lives, a reminder of the enduring strength of family and the beauty of embracing the unknown. Though the path ahead was uncertain, they faced it with courage and unwavering devotion, knowing that together, they could overcome any challenge.

C H A P T E R   1 7

Marytza's Journeys of the Astral Nomad

In the quiet solitude of her home, Marytza found herself in a peculiar state of mind. A sense of detachment enveloped her, as if her consciousness were drifting away from the confines of her physical body. With a gentle flutter, she realized she was separating from her corporeal form, her astral self-awakening to a world beyond the mundane.

As she ventured out into the ethereal realm, Marytza felt a profound sense of freedom. No longer bound by the limitations of flesh and bone, she floated effortlessly through the air, guided by an unseen force. With each passing moment, the world around her shimmered with vibrant colors and pulsating energy. In this transcendent state, Marytza discovered a newfound ability to communicate in languages she had never spoken before. Words flowed effortlessly from her lips, carrying messages of peace and understanding to all who crossed her path. She marveled at the beauty of this universal language, one that transcended the barriers of culture and nationality.

As she drifted through the astral plane, Marytza encountered beings from all corners of the globe. Faces of diverse races and ethnicities smiled warmly at her, their eyes reflecting a shared sense of wonder and curiosity. From Asia to Africa, from India to Europe, each encounter brought with it a deeper understanding of the interconnectedness of all living things. Among the souls she encountered, Marytza found kindred spirits who shared her thirst for knowledge and adventure. Together, they traversed the boundless expanse of the astral realm, exploring hidden realms and ancient mysteries that lay beyond the reach of mortal sight.

With each step, they forged bonds of friendship that transcended the boundaries of time and space. But amidst the wonders of the astral plane, Marytza also encountered pockets of darkness and despair. Lingering shadows whispered tales of sorrow and suffering, their voices echoing through the void like distant cries in the night. Though she was tempted to turn away, Marytza knew that her journey was not yet complete. With courage in her heart, she pressed on, determined to bring light to the darkest corners of the cosmos.

Guided by an inner compass of wisdom and intuition, Marytza embarked on a quest to heal the wounds of the astral realm. With each act of kindness and compassion, she dispelled the shadows of fear and ignorance that threatened to engulf the world. Through her words and deeds, she became a beacon of hope for all who sought refuge in the light. And, as her journey ended, Marytza felt a profound sense of gratitude for the experiences that had shaped her soul. Though she knew that her time in the astral realm was fleeting, she carried with her the lessons she had learned and the memories she had cherished. With a final glance at the infinite expanse of the cosmos, she bid farewell to her astral companions, knowing that their paths would one day cross again.

Returning to her physical body, Marytza felt a renewed sense of purpose and clarity. Though the world around her remained unchanged, she knew that she had been forever transformed by her journey through the astral plane. With a smile on her lips and a song in her heart, she stepped forward into the unknown, ready to embrace whatever adventures awaited her on the horizon. And so, the tale of Marytza, the astral nomad, came to an end. But her spirit lived on, forever entwined with the fabric of the universe itself. For in the vast expanse of time and space, there are no beginnings or endings, only infinite possibilities waiting to be explored.

As Marytza emerged from her university waiting room, the chatter of her friends immediately drew her attention. With an eager smile, she joined their circle, the excitement palpable in the air. As they exchanged greetings, Marytza's eyes gleamed with anticipation, hinting at the extraordinary tale she was about to share. With a theatrical flourish, she began recounting the details of her dream, each word weaving a vivid tapestry of wonder and fascination.

"It was unlike any dream I've ever had," Marytza began, her voice tinged with a mix of awe and disbelief. "I felt like I had two bodies, existing simultaneously in different realms." Her friends leaned in, captivated by her words, hanging on to every syllable as if it held the key to unlocking a profound mystery.

"Imagine," Marytza continued, her gestures animated as she painted a picture with her words, "feeling the warmth of the sun on one hand, while the cool embrace of moonlight caresses the other. It was surreal, yet undeniably real in its intensity."

Her friends exchanged intrigued glances; their curiosity piqued by the sheer strangeness of her experience. "But how did it feel?" one of them asked, unable to contain their fascination.

"It's hard to describe," Marytza admitted, her expression thoughtful as she searched for the right words to convey the ineffable sensation. "It was as if I was both weightless and grounded, existing in a state of perfect equilibrium. And the emotions...oh, the emotions were unlike anything I've ever felt before. A kaleidoscope of joy, wonder, and a hint of apprehension, all swirling together in a dizzying whirlwind."

Her friends nodded in understanding; their imaginations sparked by Marytza's vivid descriptions. "Listen," she said, her voice lowering to a conspiratorial whisper, "this is an extraordinary and inexplicable thing. But somehow, amidst the strangeness, there was a sense of profound connection, as if I had glimpsed the true nature of reality itself."

As Marytza's tale ended, her friends sat in awed silence, the weight of her words lingering in the air like a tantalizing enigma waiting to be unraveled. And though they may never fully comprehend the mysteries of her dream, they were grateful for the glimpse into a world beyond the confines of their own imagination. For in that fleeting moment, they had touched something magical, something wondrous, something that defied explanation yet resonated deep within their souls.

CHAPTER 18

The Vision of Underground Nicky's Conditioned PARTNER

In the dimly lit underground chamber, the air hung heavy with anticipation as Nicky's conditioned partner, with her piercing gaze, recounted her vivid vision. She stood between her albino parents, who had come to visit Nicky's father, the patriarch of their clandestine community. Here, Marytza, the daughter with an otherworldly aura, addressed Nicky's father, her impatience evident in her trembling voice. "My darling," he responded, his voice a soothing balm, "patience is a virtue." Marytza persisted, revealing the strange and unsettling visions that plagued her.

Nicky's father, a figure of wisdom and authority, reassured Marytza that her fiancé would soon come to her aid. "A little patience, princess of the lands," he gently chided, his words carrying the weight of both comfort and command. And, during their conversation, the albino couple and Nicky's parents, began to move gracefully in a dance that echoed the ancient choreography of their Haitian roots. Their movements were fluid, mesmerizing, as if channeling the spirits of their ancestors.

The dance unfolded in the flickering candlelight, casting shadows that danced along the walls like specters from a bygone era. Each step, each gesture, spoke volumes of a culture rich in tradition and mystery. And, As the dance reached its crescendo, Marytza's eyes widened in awe, her visions momentarily forgotten in the face of such beauty and grace. For a fleeting moment, the weight of her burdens lifted, replaced by the simple joy of witnessing something truly magical. At that moment, Nicky's father, observing the scene with a knowing smile, nodded in silent approval. In this underground sanctuary, where secrets were whispered and dreams took flight, the dance served as a reminder of the resilience of the human spirit.

With the dance concluded, a sense of tranquility settled over the chamber, a rare moment of peace amidst the chaos of their existence. Nicky's father turned to Marytza once more, his words carrying the weight of prophecy. "Your fiancé will come soon to find you," he assured her, his voice echoing with certainty. And though the path ahead was fraught with uncertainty, Marytza took solace in the knowledge that she was not alone. And so, in the depths of the underground, amidst shadows and whispers, the vision of Nicky's conditioned partner offered a glimpse of hope—a beacon of light in the darkness, guiding them towards an uncertain future.

CHAPTER 19

Serendipitous Encounters

Marytza and her parents ventured to a lavish restaurant for a delightful evening. As they settled in and began relishing their meal, an unexpected guest, Nicky, joined them. The exchange of glances between Marytza and Nicky ignited a spark of curiosity. The crossing of their gazes, they look at each other and smile, Marytza's mom asks her "what is the matter", and she answers, "I'm ok". She was smiling at him so much she must have dropped her tea on her and she whistles him a kiss from the bottom of her hand and gestures Nicky's name with the gesture of her mouth. And the same with Nicky's mom when she questions him, what's going on while he makes the girl's name with the gestures of his mouth. Caught in a moment of silent communication, masking the true nature of their connection. With a playful gesture, Marytza teased Nicky, who reciprocated with a secret sign of acknowledgment. Their silent communication spoke volumes, hidden from the prying eyes of their parents.

Marytza and her parents leave and thereafter Nicky leaves with his mother and follows them without the knowledge of his mother who sees him abnormally funny, he says, "Mom you see sometimes I like to change my mind when I drive". Seizing an opportunity, Nicky veered off course during their journey home, much to his mother's amusement. His innocent pretext concealed his true motive — to catch a glimpse of Marytza's abode.

In the quiet of the night, Marytza's neighborhood witnessed an unexpected visitor. Nicky's impromptu decision led him on a journey fueled by curiosity and a hint of infatuation. As Nicky stealthily observed Marytza's residence from a distance, he couldn't shake the feeling of exhilaration. Serendipity had intertwined their lives, guiding them towards an unforeseen connection.

Lost in the moment, Marytza and Nicky embarked on a journey filled with uncertainty and possibility. Their chance encounter blossomed into a newfound friendship, bound by shared glances and secret smiles. Though separated by the night, Marytza and Nicky's hearts remained tethered by the invisible thread of fate. Their clandestine connection hinted at a future filled with endless possibilities.

As dawn broke, Marytza and Nicky's paths diverged once more. Yet, the memory of their serendipitous encounter lingered, a testament to the unpredictable nature of destiny and the joy found in unexpected connections.

CHAPTER 20

Angelic Encounter

Nicky felt an inexplicable sensation coursing through his body as he found himself doubling up, his ethereal form taking flight with wings unfurled like those of an angel. With purpose in his heart, he soared toward Marytza's house, guided by an unseen force drawing him to her.

Arriving at Marytza's window, Nicky beheld her serene form, her astral body shimmering beside her physical vessel. Together, they embarked on a journey, their souls intertwining as they embarked on a romantic walk under the moonlit sky. They traversed through an evening landscape bathed in a hushed serenity. A realm untouched by the clamor of the world. In this tranquil haven, they found solace in each other's presence, their hearts beating in synchrony with the rhythm of the universe. As they strolled along the silent streets, Nicky felt compelled to express the depths of his feelings for Marytza. Pausing beneath the canopy of stars, he recited a poem that had been born from the depths of his soul, a testament to their timeless connection.

"In the depth of the night," he began, his voice carrying the weight of his emotions. "When we're lonely, our dreams easily come true. My heart is full of emotions, full of chills. The evening breeze and the smell of roses are enough to trigger happiness."

"In the depth of the night," Nicky continued, his words imbued with a sense of profound truth. "Fame and fortune are negligible. They define themselves as the goodness of the heart. And walk how wind and perfume of flowers. Just love and be loved. The world and sin are misunderstood."

In that moment, amidst the stillness of the night, Nicky and Marytza existed in a realm beyond time and space, their souls dancing in harmony to the melody of love's eternal song. And as the night waned on, they knew that their bond was unbreakable, destined to endure through the ages.

In the depth of the night, where silence reigns supreme,
As mysterious as the depths of a heart's dream.
Love blooms, a boundless joy unfurled,
Divine grace, a shield in this earthly world.

They kiss and they entwine, passion's fiery embrace,
A love painted in hues of roses, in tender grace.
Their love scene unfolds, a tale untold.

CHAPTER 21

The Awakening: Maritza's Journey to Reclaiming Herself

The morning dawned and Marytza stirred in her sleep as a gentle hand shook her awake. Blinking away the remnants of dreams, her mother roused her and stood by her bedside, concern etched on her face. The tranquility of the moment was shattered by the resurgence of a haunting memory. As the haze of sleep lifted, Marytza's mind became clearer, yet something felt amiss. She felt a surge of unease wash over her. It was as if a shadow had descended upon her soul, casting doubt and insecurity where confidence once dwelled.

Her astral recollections flooded back disrupting her peace; a stark reminder of a past she had fought so hard to overcome.

As Marytza grappled with the weight of her rekindled trauma, the harsh reality of her present circumstance pierced through the fog of her subconscious. With a sinking heart, she came to the agonizing realization that she had lost something integral to her identity, something deeply intertwined with her sense of womanhood; she had lost one of her eyes – a cruel testament to the trials she had endured and the sacrifices she had made along her journey. The weight of this loss pressed down on her, threatening to engulf her in despair.

In the solitude of her bedroom, Marytza confronted the raw emotions swirling within her. The ache of her loss reverberated through her being. Unable to ignore the turmoil within her, she embarked on a quest for understanding. During her moment of darkness, a flicker of resilience ignited within her soul, a defiant spark refusing to be extinguished by adversity. She sought solace in ancient texts and wise elders, hoping to unlock the secrets of her astral and reclaim what was rightfully hers. With each step forward, she delved deeper into the mysteries of her own existence.

With steely determination, Marytza resolved to embrace her newfound reality with courage and grace. Though the road ahead may be fraught with challenges and uncertainties, she vowed to face each obstacle head-on, drawing strength from the depths of her spirit and the unwavering support of her loved ones. She faced the darkest corners of her soul, unearthing buried traumas and confronting painful truths. Through tears and triumphs alike, she remained steadfast in her pursuit of healing and self-discovery.

In the wake of her revelation, Marytza emerged from the depths of despair, her spirit tempered by adversity and fortified by the resilience of the human spirit. Though scarred by the wounds of her past, she stood tall, a beacon of hope and inspiration to all who dared to confront their demons and emerge victorious against all odds. In the midst of her struggle, she learned the power of vulnerability. She allowed herself to feel the depths of her pain without shame or reservation, embracing every facet of her being with compassion and acceptance. In doing so, she found strength in her vulnerability, emerging stronger than before.

As Marytza journeyed further into the heart of her identity, she began to rediscover the essence of her womanhood. With each revelation, she pieced together the fragments of her shattered self, weaving them into a tapestry of resilience and grace. In reclaiming her womanhood, she reclaimed her power.

Through mindfulness and self-care, Marytza embarked on the path to healing. She nurtured her body, mind, and spirit with love and tenderness, honoring the sacredness of her journey. With each passing day, she felt the wounds of the past gradually heal, leaving behind scars that bore witness to her strength.

As the fog of uncertainty lifted, she emerged from the depths of her despair, reborn and renewed. With a newfound sense of purpose and clarity, she faced the world with confidence and conviction. Though her journey was far from over, she walked forward with courage, knowing that she was no longer defined by her past. In the depths of her soul, she knew that true empowerment lay not in the destination, but in the endless pursuit of self-discovery and growth. And so, with head held high and heart ablaze, she stepped boldly into the unknown, ready to embrace whatever lay ahead.

CHAPTER 22

Nicky's revelation

Fearing the worst, Nicky prepared himself for a confrontation, steeling his resolve as he ventured into the unknown. But as he turned a corner, he was greeted not by a fearsome adversary, but by a figure bathed in light, its features obscured by a shimmering veil of energy.

As the figure stepped forward, the veil dissolved, revealing a face that sent shivers down Nicky's spine. It was him, but not him, a distorted reflection of his own image cast against the canvas of the astral plane.

Confusion clouded Nicky's thoughts as he struggled to make sense of the surreal encounter. Who was this doppelganger, and what did it want with him?

But before he could voice his questions, the figure spoke, its voice echoing through the void with a resonance that seemed to shake the very fabric of reality.

"Nicky," it said, its words both familiar and foreign, "you have been chosen to wield a power beyond your wildest dreams, a power that will shape the destiny of worlds."

With a sense of trepidation, Nicky listened as the figure revealed the true nature of his transformation, recounting ancient prophecies and forgotten legends that spoke of a chosen one destined to bring balance to the astral realm.

But as the weight of his newfound destiny settled upon his shoulders, Nicky felt a surge of determination coursing through him, driving him to accept the challenge that lay before him.

With the guidance of his astral mentor, Nicky embarked on a series of trials designed to test his courage and strength, each more perilous than the last. From navigating treacherous mazes to facing off against fearsome adversaries, Nicky pushed himself to the limit, drawing upon reserves of power he never knew he possessed.

But amidst the trials and tribulations, a darker force began to stir, its presence lurking in the shadows like a hungry predator waiting to strike. Seductive whispers echoed through the corridors of Nicky's mind, tempting him with promises of untold power and glory.

At first, Nicky resisted the allure of the darkness, clinging to the light with unwavering resolve. But as the trials grew more arduous and the stakes higher, doubt crept into his heart, sowing seeds of discord that threatened to tear him apart from within.

Fearing the consequences of his weakness, Nicky sought solace in the wisdom of his mentor, but even their guidance proved powerless against the insidious influence of the shadow.

In a moment of weakness, Nicky succumbed to the temptations of the darkness, striking a Faustian bargain that would forever alter the course of his destiny. With each passing moment, he felt himself slipping further and further into the abyss, his soul consumed by the very power he had sought to wield.

But even as he embraced the darkness, a glimmer of hope remained, a flickering flame that refused to be extinguished. With the last vestiges of his strength,

Nicky fought against the tide of corruption, clinging to the light with a tenacity born of desperation.

In the end, it was not his strength or his courage that saved him, but his capacity for love. In the depths of his despair, Nicky found redemption in the selfless act of sacrifice, offering up his own life to save those he held dear.

As the darkness receded, Nicky found himself standing on the precipice of oblivion, his astral form battered and broken, but his spirit unbroken. With a sense of clarity that had eluded him for so long, he embraced his true purpose, vowing to use his newfound power to protect the innocent and uphold the values he held dear.

With each step he took, Nicky felt a sense of renewal washing over him, a second chance at redemption that he would not squander. And though the road ahead would be fraught with peril, he faced it with a newfound sense of purpose and determination, ready to confront whatever challenges awaited him.

In the years that followed, Nicky became a legend, his name whispered in awe by those who had witnessed his exploits firsthand. But amidst the tales of heroism and bravery, few knew the true extent of his sacrifice, the price he had paid to save the world from the brink of destruction.

But Nicky did not seek recognition or glory, content to walk the path of the humble hero, serving as a beacon of hope for those in need. And though his journey had been fraught with hardship and sorrow, he knew that it had been worth it, for he had found true purpose in the service of others.

CHAPTER 23

Nicky's astral body experience: a sexual orgasm

As Nicky's astral body stirred from slumber, it found itself back at home. His eyes fluttered open, his surroundings unfamiliar yet strangely comforting. As he sat up, he realized he was in his own room, bathed in the soft glow of dawn filtering through the curtains. Confusion clouded his mind as he tried to piece together the events of the previous night. The transition from the ethereal realm to the material planet was seamless, as if Nicky had never left. As consciousness flooded back into his astral form, Nicky's senses sharpened, and he became acutely aware of the subtle energies that permeated the space around him. The room seemed to pulsate with life, as though every object within it held a secret whisper of the universe's mysteries.

Slowly, he became aware of a dampness beneath him, and his heart skipped a beat as he looked down to see his sheets stained with an all too familiar substance. Embarrassment flooded his cheeks as he realized what had happened. How could he have lost control like this? As Nicky struggled to comprehend the surreal experience, he couldn't shake the feeling that something was different, something had changed. It was as if a veil had been lifted from his perception, revealing a world he had never before noticed.

Unable to ignore the strange sensations coursing through him, Nicky tentatively reached out, his hand passing effortlessly through the bedside table. Shock coursed through him as he realized he was no longer bound by the limitations of his physical form. He was... astral. With newfound curiosity, Nicky explored his surroundings, drifting through walls and ceilings with ease. He marveled at the freedom of his ethereal form, reveling in the sensation of weightlessness that enveloped him.

But amidst the wonder, a nagging question tugged at the corners of his mind: why had this happened to him? What had triggered this strange transformation?

As Nicky pondered these questions, memories of the previous night began to surface, fragmented and disjointed. He remembered a sense of unease, a feeling of being watched, but the details eluded him like grains of sand slipping through his fingers.

Determined to unravel the mystery, Nicky set out on a quest for answers, his astral form gliding effortlessly through the streets of his hometown. With each passing moment, he felt more attuned to the subtle energies pulsating through the fabric of reality, as if he were tapping into a primal source of knowledge that lay dormant within him.

As Nicky delved deeper into the mysteries of the astral realm, he became aware of a presence lurking on the fringes of his consciousness, a shadowy figure that seemed to be watching his every move with a mixture of curiosity and amusement.

While he took in his surroundings, he felt a gentle warmth wash over him, a sensation that transcended physical touch and resonated deep within his soul. It was as if the very essence of love itself had enveloped him, wrapping him in its tender embrace. And then, as if guided by an unseen force, Nicky's gaze fell upon a figure standing before him, bathed in a soft, ethereal glow.

It was her – the one whose presence had haunted Nicky's dreams and filled his waking thoughts with longing. In that moment, time seemed to stand still as their eyes locked in a silent exchange of understanding and recognition. There were no words needed between them, for their hearts spoke a language that transcended the limitations of speech.

In the hushed intimacy of the room, Nicky and his ethereal companion moved closer to one another, drawn together by an irresistible magnetic pull. Their spirits danced in harmony, entwining and merging until they became one, bound by a love that defied the boundaries of time and space. And then, as if by some divine decree, the room faded away, and Nicky found himself standing in a vast, open field bathed in the soft glow of moonlight. The air was filled with the heady scent of wildflowers, and the sound of gentle breezes whispered through the tall grass.

Hand in hand, Nicky and his beloved wandered through the moonlit meadow, their laughter echoing across the expanse of the night. With each step they took, they felt more alive than ever before, their souls soaring on the wings of love and ecstasy. As they reached the crest of a gentle hill, they came to a stop, their eyes drawn to the breathtaking panorama spread out before them. Below, a tranquil lake shimmered in the moonlight, its surface reflecting the countless stars that adorned the night sky.

Without a word, they descended the hillside, their footsteps soft against the dew-kissed grass. At the water's edge, they paused, their reflections merging in the mirror-like surface of the lake. Then, as if in a trance, they stepped into the cool embrace of the water, letting it envelop them in its liquid embrace. For a timeless moment, they swam together beneath the starlit sky, their bodies entwined in a graceful ballet of love and desire. And as they emerged from the water, their spirits soared ever higher, their hearts beating as one in the eternal rhythm of love.

As the first light of dawn broke across the horizon, they found themselves back in the sanctuary of their astral realm, their bodies entwined in a loving embrace. And as they drifted off to sleep once more, they knew that their love would endure for all eternity, a beacon of light in the darkness of the cosmos.

CHAPTER 24

The Unraveling Dream

As Marytza lay interned in the sterile hospital ward, her mother, fraught with worry, relayed the concerning details to the doctor. Amidst the somber atmosphere, conversations swirled about the possibility of rousing someone from deep slumber. "She had blood in her underclothes and skirt," her mother exclaimed, incredulous at the sight. Further examinations unveiled Marytza's condition, she was in full belt.

The topic of her sexual experiences arose between Marytza and her doctor. The doctor, seeking honesty, gently probed Marytza about her intimate life. Marytza, bewildered, confessed to only experiencing such encounters in dreams.

Marytza's father, a steadfast pastor, entered the room; his presence seemed almost out of place. Filled with agitation, he addressed his daughter, asserting the gravity of the situation. "You are beautiful and very pregnant," he declared, "despite the fact that you have received the fruit of your bowels in the world, we as responsible parents and we do not demand anything from you, if only the identity of the father of your baby" urging her to reveal the identity to avoid the ire of their religious community. "I am ready to manage with this boy and his parents for a contrary marriage" the father continued "I had a feeling that you had known the boy from the last time at the restaurant. You say you haven't had intimacy - now you say you remember a dream, listen if young girls could be pregnant in a dream, I would have a thousand sons and daughters, because everyone had sweaty dreams , today I have just repeated the experience even though your mother would have been very close to me, according to what you say Holy Virgin Mary, men who are taken by the moving charms of a girl no longer have only to be done, no more question of sending flowers, courting the one we love, we see her we are going somewhere, we are looking for a place in our own dream to lie down and boom-boom Christ will be born"

Amidst the tension, Marytza recounted her dream encounters, unable to fathom the reality of her circumstances. Her father, incredulous, dismissed her claims, citing the absurdity of dreams leading to pregnancy.

Emotions ran high as Marytza's mother wept inconsolably, while her father grappled with the implausible situation. The doctor intervened, urging calm and seeking to understand the complexities at play.

In a private conversation with Marytza's father, the doctor urged him to engage with his daughter and seek the truth from her perspective. "You know that today's young people are small in spirit. You should talk to your daughter instead" the doctor said. However, the father remained skeptical, dismissing Marytza's account as mere jest.

In a final exchange, the father conveyed his skepticism to the doctor "If women could be pregnant in dreams, those who have the feathers in their hands would be legitimate fathers and the world would be too small for all these people, what she says is pure joke", emphasizing the absurdity of dreams leading to conception. Amidst the uncertainty, one thing remained clear: the need for understanding and compassion in navigating this surreal ordeal.

CHAPTER 25

The Revelation of Eros

Marytza lay upon the sterile hospital bed, her heart heavy with sorrow and uncertainty. The harsh fluorescent lights cast stark shadows across the room, amplifying the whispers of doubt that surrounded her like a suffocating fog. Everyone doubted her pregnancy, casting judgment upon her innocence. But amidst the darkness of her despair, a glimmer of hope emerged in the form of a dream.

In the depths of her slumber, Marytza found herself transported to a realm of ethereal beauty. There, standing before her, was Eros, the god of love, radiant and resplendent in all his divine glory. His presence filled her with a sense of peace and tranquility, banishing the doubts and fears that had plagued her waking hours.

With a gentle smile, Eros extended his hand towards Marytza, offering her a bouquet of pure white flowers. Their petals shimmered with an otherworldly light, filling the room with their celestial fragrance. At the feet of Eros stood the naked Nicky, their bodies sculpted like marble, each holding a bouquet of white flowers in their hands.

As Eros spoke, his voice was like music to Marytza's ears, soothing her troubled soul with its melodic cadence. He spoke of love in its purest form, of the sacred bond that unites two souls in perfect harmony. His words resonated with Marytza, filling her with a sense of clarity and understanding. "Dear Marytza, I have come to bring you a message of hope and reassurance." Eros began, his voice echoing through the chamber, "I am Eros, the god of love, one of the constructive forces of the cosmos. Since the dawn of time, I have remained unchanged, a symbol of pure love in a world tainted by greed and corruption."

Eros spoke of his eternal vigilance over the lovers of the world, guiding them towards true happiness and fulfillment. He lamented the perversion of love in the modern age, where it had been reduced to nothing more than a transaction, a commodity to be bought and sold.

"But fear not, dear Marytza," Eros continued, his gaze unwavering, "for true love still exists in this world, waiting to be discovered by those who dare to follow the beating of their hearts. It is a love that transcends boundaries and defies convention, a love that knows no limits." With these words, Eros turned to the naked Nicky, their eyes filled with devotion and reverence. In a solemn procession, they knelt before Marytza's bed, their hands outstretched in offering. Marytza felt a surge of warmth and gratitude wash over her, filling her heart with newfound hope.

"For you, dear Marytza," Eros declared, his voice resounding with power and authority, "I promise protection and guidance, for your journey is fraught with challenges and dangers. But know this, very early tomorrow, your son's father will come to see your parents to ask for your hand in marriage."

As the vision faded and Marytza awoke from her dream, she felt a renewed sense of purpose and resolve coursing through her veins. She took comfort in believing that she was not alone, that the gods themselves watched over her with benevolent eyes. And so, with a heart full of hope and a spirit unbroken, Marytza prepared to face whatever trials lay ahead, guided by the wisdom of Eros and the promise of true love.

CHAPTER 26

Declarations and Revelations

The following day after Eros' visit to Marytza, Nicky stood at her doorstep, his heart pounding with nervous anticipation. In his hand, he held a bouquet of pristine white flowers, a symbol of purity and sincerity. With each step closer to the door, his resolve strengthened. This moment would change everything. As Marytza opened the door, her eyes widened in surprise at the sight of Nicky standing before her, flowers in hand. He took a deep breath, summoning the courage to speak the words he had rehearsed countless times in his mind.

"Marytza," Nicky began, his voice trembling slightly, "I need to tell you something important. These flowers... they're for you. But they're not just flowers. They're a symbol of my love, my commitment, my responsibility." Marytza's confusion turned to curiosity as Nicky continued, his words flowing from his heart. "You see, Marytza, these flowers represent more than just a gesture of affection. They represent a promise—a promise to stand by you, to support you, to be there for you and our baby."

A gasp escaped Marytza's lips as she processed Nicky's declaration. Her eyes filled with emotion as she realized the depth of his words. This was not just a romantic gesture; it was a profound statement of dedication and devotion.

"I... I don't know what to say," Marytza stammered, overcome with emotion.

Nicky reached out, gently placing the bouquet in her hands. "You don't have to say anything," he said softly. "Just know that I'm here for you, no matter what. We're in this together."

Just then, the door behind Marytza swung open, revealing Nicky's mom standing in the doorway, her expression a mix of surprise and pride. She had arrived at the perfect moment, witnessing her son's heartfelt declaration.

"Nicky," she said, her voice choked with emotion, "I had no idea... I'm so proud of you, son."

Tears welled up in Nicky's eyes as he embraced his mom, feeling a sense of relief and validation wash over him. In that moment, surrounded by the two most important women in his life, he knew he had made the right choice. As they stood there, wrapped in each other's arms, Nicky couldn't help but feel a sense of hope for the future. Whatever challenges lay ahead, he was ready to face them, knowing that he had the love and support of his family by his side.

CHAPTER 27
A Wedding Amidst Nature's SYMPHONIES

In the quaint village of Sunvale, Nicky and Marytza stood at the altar, ready to embark on the journey of marriage. The church was adorned with flowers of every color and elegant decorations, creating a breathtaking backdrop for the ceremony which exuded an aura of celebration, anticipation, and love. As the horn concert filled the air, every pew was filled with friends, family and guests eagerly awaiting the union of the couple.

Suddenly, a miraculous sight unfolded outside as if in divine approval casting its colorful glow over the ceremony. A rainbow appeared against the canvas of a sunny afternoon, casting its colorful hues over the church, seemingly blessing the union with its presence. Thereafter, the sunny afternoon was momentarily interrupted by the arrival of a thunderstorm, adding an unexpected twist to the proceedings. Undeterred by the storm, Nicky and Marytza exchanged vows, their love shining through the chaos.

With thunder rumbling in the background, they were pronounced husband and wife, their bond strengthened by their unwavering commitment to each other, their love unwavering in the face of nature's fury. The thunderstorm raged outside, its intensity matching the passion of their love. Despite the challenges they faced, their love prevailed, a testament to the resilience of the human spirit. As they kissed for the first time as husband and wife, the storm outside seemed to relent, acknowledging the power of their love.

And as the storm passed, leaving behind a glistening rainbow, the church erupted into cheers and applause. Friends and family gathered around the newlyweds, showering them with love and congratulations Nicky and Marytza emerged from the church hand in hand, ready to face whatever challenges life may bring. And so, amidst the beauty of nature's symphony, Nicky and Marytza embarked on the journey of marriage, their love shining brightly like the rainbow that had blessed their union, resilient in the face of any storm that may come their way.

After the wedding, all in attendance continued the celebration at the reception. Nicky stood in the luxuriously adorned room, marveling at the opulence surrounding him. The room was a testament to lavishness, adorned with lovingly crafted decorations that spoke of care and attention to detail. Tables groaned under the weight of drinks of all kinds, dishes representing cuisines from around the world, and an array of cakes that could satisfy any sweet tooth.

But as the festivities unfolded, an eerie shift occurred. The wines in the glasses turned to blood, and strange creatures appeared within them. Animals of all kinds wriggled and swam amidst the crimson liquid, causing murmurs of confusion and alarm among the guests. Cakes, once delectable treats, revealed themselves to be infested with worms, frogs, and other unsettling creatures. The air seemed thick with an unseen presence, and Nicky could not shake the feeling of unease that settled over him.

Suddenly, the room was teeming with spiders, crawling along the walls and ceilings, their presence casting a sinister shadow over the celebration. Panic rippled through the crowd as guests recoiled in horror, unable to comprehend the surreal spectacle unfolding before them.

Then, just as abruptly as it began, the hallucination shattered. Nicky blinked, his mind struggling to grasp the reality of what had just transpired. With a deep breath, he pulled himself together, the disorienting haze lifting as clarity returned.

As the scene dissolved into normalcy, Nicky found solace in the arms of his beloved. Beneath the gentle cascade of water from a shower, they embraced, the love between them was like roses in full bloom. And as they embarked on their honeymoon journey, the memory of the surreal reception faded into the past, replaced by the promise of a future filled with love and laughter.

CHAPTER 28

The Dreamscape Revelations

As the moon cast its gentle glow upon the newlyweds, Marytza lay beside Nicky, her physical beauty illuminated by the soft light filtering through the curtains. The cameras captured every detail, every curve of her form, as if preserving the moment for eternity. Their love was palpable, an extraordinary journey that had led them to this serene moment.

Nicky drifted into a deep sleep; his mind traversing realms unknown. In the depths of his subconscious, a surreal scene unfolded. Twins, with bald heads and unclothed bodies, appeared before him, their presence ominous yet strangely familiar. With ethereal grace, the twins lifted Nicky from his bed and carried him into a world shrouded in mystery. As they journeyed through the abyss of his mind, Nicky felt a sense of foreboding creeping over him. What awaited him in this enigmatic realm?

In the recesses of his dream, echoes of his father's world reverberated. Nicky sensed a connection, a link to his past that had long been buried beneath layers of forgotten memories. Was this journey a reckoning with his lineage, a confrontation with his own identity?

As they reached their destination, Nicky found himself standing before a tribunal of shadowy figures. Eyes scrutinized him, weighing his very essence against an unseen scale of judgment. What had he done to warrant such scrutiny, such condemnation? In the hushed whispers of the tribunal, Nicky's true nature was laid bare. The pact from which he was born, the legacy of his lineage, unfolded before him like a dark tapestry woven with threads of destiny. Was he merely a pawn in a cosmic game, or did he possess the power to shape his own fate?

With each revelation, Nicky felt the weight of his existence pressing down upon him. The shadows that lurked within his soul now danced in the spotlight of truth, their tendrils reaching out to ensnare him in their grasp. Would he succumb to the darkness, or would he find the strength to defy his predetermined destiny?

As the trial reached its climax, Nicky stood at a crossroads, torn between the echoes of his past and the possibilities of his future. The twins, silent witnesses to his inner turmoil, awaited his decision anxiously. Would he embrace his heritage, or would he forge a new path untethered by the chains of fate?

With a jolt, Nicky awoke from his dream, his heart racing with the echoes of his subconscious journey. Beside him, Marytza stirred, her presence a beacon of light in the darkness that had enveloped him. As he gazed upon her sleeping form, he realized that the power to shape his destiny lay not in the hands of fate, but within his own heart.

Simultaneously, the night enveloped Marytza in its inky embrace, her mind wandered into the realms of the surreal. Dreams, or perhaps nightmares, unfurled before her like dark tapestries woven from the fabric of her deepest fears.

In this twisted vision, she found herself ensnared by a grotesque tableau of suffering. Wounds marred her flesh, their jagged edges a testament to some unseen violence inflicted upon her form. Her once vibrant locks were now naught but a memory, leaving her scalp barren and exposed to the cruel whims of the elements.

But it was not just the physical toll that weighed heavily upon her; her very essence seemed to wither under the weight of this nightmarish ordeal. Her feet, swollen and distorted, betrayed the strain of an unseen burden, while her body, shrunken and emaciated, bore the scars of a relentless assault on her very being.

And then there was the blood. Viscous and dark, it poured forth from her lips in a torrent of anguish, staining her lips and tongue with its bitter taste. Each retch brought forth a fresh wave of terror, a reminder of the fragility of her mortal shell.

As the dream reached its crescendo, Marytza awoke with a start, her heart pounding like a drumbeat of dread. Beside her, her companion stirred, roused from their slumber by the palpable aura of fear that hung heavy in the air.

For a moment, they simply lay there, caught in the tangled web of their own thoughts. But as the echoes of the dream faded into the recesses of memory, they found solace in the reassuring presence of one another, a beacon of light amid the darkness.

And though the specter of the dream still lingered, casting its long shadow over their waking hours, they knew that together they would find the strength to face whatever trials lay ahead. For in the crucible of adversity, their bond would be forged anew, a testament to the resilience of the human spirit in the face of adversity.

With newfound resolve, they both embraced the dawn of a new day, ready to confront whatever trials lay ahead. They individually knew that the journey of self-discovery was far from over. Ny each other's side, they would face the unknown with courage, knowing that their love would guide them through the darkest of nights.

CHAPTER 29

A Gathering Turned Nightmare: Nicky's Apoplexy

The following day, close relatives and friends gathered in a secondary celebration of Nicky and Marytza's union. They congregated around the table, laughing, and sharing stories, their spirits high as they enjoyed a hearty meal together. Suddenly, amidst the chatter and clinking of utensils, Nicky collapsed to the ground, writhing in agony, foam forming at the corners of their mouths. Shock rippled through the room as everyone turned their attention to Nicky's distress. Ultimately, Panic surged as loved ones rushed to Nicky's side, their faces etched with worry and fear. Some cried out for help, while others instinctively began to pray, seeking solace in their faith during this moment of crisis.

Someone dialed for emergency medical assistance, desperately pleading for help as they described Nicky's condition to the dispatcher. Time seemed to stand still as the group anxiously awaited the arrival of medical professionals, their hearts heavy with concern for Nicky's well-being. Despite the frantic prayers and efforts of those gathered, Nicky's condition remained unchanged, their body still convulsing uncontrollably on the ground.

As the minutes stretched into what felt like an eternity, a sense of helplessness settled over the room, each person grappling with their own feelings of fear and uncertainty. Finally, the sound of sirens pierced the air, signaling the arrival of paramedics who quickly sprang into action, their skilled hands working to stabilize Nicky and transport them to the hospital. Here, With Nicky now in the hands of medical professionals, the group gathered in a solemn circle, offering prayers of hope and support for their beloved friend or family member as they faced an uncertain future.

And so, the evening that began with laughter and camaraderie took a sudden and unexpected turn, leaving those presents forever changed by the sobering reminder of life's fragility and the importance of cherishing each moment with those we hold dear.

As the evening sun dipped below the horizon, casting long shadows across the room, Marytza sat beside Nicky's bed, her heart heavy with worry. Nicky lay there, his once vibrant spirit now subdued, lost in the grip of a mysterious ailment.

"She shakes him, saying 'don't do that, Honey,'" Marytza murmured softly, her voice trembling with emotion. She reached out to touch him, hoping to rouse him from his slumber, but Nicky remained still, his breaths shallow and laboring.

Desperation clawed at Marytza's chest as she brought a steaming cup of tea to Nicky's lips, hoping to revive him with its warmth. She stroked his hair gently, her fingers tracing invisible patterns on his forehead, willing him to wake from his troubled sleep.

In a desperate attempt to bring joy back into Nicky's life, Marytza fetched her guitar and began to play a sweet melody, the notes dancing through the air like whispers of hope. But even the music failed to stir Nicky from his trance, his body limp and unresponsive.

Tears welled up in Marytza's eyes as she realized the gravity of the situation. Panic seized her heart as she called out for help, her cries echoing off the walls of the room, desperate to break through the silence that enveloped them.

With trembling hands and a voice choked with emotion, Marytza began to recite Psalm 8, her words a prayer of anguish and supplication. She clung to her faith like a lifeline, seeking solace during her despair, as she watched helplessly over Nicky, her beloved, her heart breaking with each passing moment.

And as the night stretched on, Marytza remained by Nicky's side, her love a beacon of hope in the darkness, refusing to let go, even as the world around them seemed to crumble.

CHAPTER 30

The Unraveling of Marytza

As Marytza plummeted through the air, the sensation of weightlessness consumed her. In that fleeting moment, she felt a sense of freedom juxtaposed with impending doom. She reached out, grasping for anything to hold onto, but found only empty air slipping through her fingers.

With a sudden impact, Marytza landed in the palms of the earth, her body splitting upon impact. Pain shot through her, yet amidst the agony, she found herself gazing at her own form, disjointed and fragile.

Desperation flooded her senses as she called out for help, her voice echoing into the vast expanse of the unknown. Her wings, once majestic and powerful, lay shattered and torn, reminiscent of a fallen angel stripped of her grace.

Through tear-blurred eyes, Marytza glanced at the figure of Nicky cradled in her arms. In that moment, despite the chaos surrounding her, a sense of determination ignited within her soul. She would rise again, reclaiming her strength and embracing the broken pieces of herself.

Marytza knew that even in the darkest depths of despair, the spirit of an angel endures, resilient and unwavering in the face of adversity.

CHAPTER 31

The Awakening IS A HALLUCINATION

In the room dedicated to the practice of white magic, Father Sébastien found solace amidst the eclectic array of sacred artifacts. The space, adorned with purposeful decoration, housed an assortment of large tomes, including the Bible, alongside chalices and scattered Ostia. A colossal crucifix dominated one corner, its imposing figure casting a protective aura over the room. Candles flickered, casting dancing shadows that whispered secrets to the attentive priest.

As Father Sébastien knelt in prayer, the air crackled with anticipation. Outside, the furious wind howled its protest, as if sensing the impending shift in the balance of power. With each fervent plea, the atmosphere grew charged, until finally, with a deafening clap of thunder, the heavens answered.

In a blinding flash of lightning, Father Sébastien felt himself torn asunder. His very essence seemed to splinter and scatter, leaving him naked and vulnerable, like an angel stripped of its celestial robes. Yet, amidst the chaos, a singular cry pierced the tumult—a cry that stirred something primal within him.

Marytza.

With a surge of newfound strength, Father Sébastien unfurled wings of pure light and soared into the stormy night. His heart pounded with a mixture of fear and determination as he raced to her side, guided by an instinctual need to protect.

But as he reached her, his senses were assaulted by a wave of unfamiliar desire. It coursed through him like wildfire, consuming reason, and restraint in its wake. Marytza stood before him, bathed in moonlight, her form ethereal and alluring. In his delirium, he saw her beckoning him with eyes that promised both salvation and damnation.

Driven by forces beyond his comprehension, Father Sébastien succumbed to the allure of the forbidden.

In that moment of weakness, he abandoned himself to the intoxicating embrace of desire, heedless of the consequences that awaited.

Little did he know, the true battle had only just begun, and the lines between salvation and sin blurred in the darkness of the night.

Father Sebastian and Marytza embarked on a journey that would intertwine fate with faith, where the ethereal met the earthly in a dance of profound significance.

The crisp evening air whispered through the streets as they made their way to the sacred grounds where Father Sebastian's calling awaited. His demeanor exuded a quiet resolve, a steadfastness born of unwavering belief.

Arriving at the church, a sanctum of solace and supplication, Father Sebastian's presence commanded the very essence of divinity. With solemn grace, he approached the font of holy water, its purity shimmering in the dim light.

As he dipped his hand into the blessed vessel, the water seemed to stir with an otherworldly energy, as if aware of its sacred purpose. With reverent precision, he clasped the rosary, a symbol of devotion and protection, around his neck, its beads a testament to the strength of his convictions.

In that moment, a hallowed alliance was forged, a union of mortal and divine, bound by a shared mission to vanquish darkness and usher in the light. For it was with this holy water, imbued with the power of faith, that the malevolent forces of the albinos would be purged from existence.

With hearts ablaze with purpose, Father Sebastian and Marytza stood united, poised to confront the shadows that lurked in the periphery of their world. Little did they know their journey was but the beginning of an odyssey that would test the very limits of their resolve and challenge the boundaries of belief itself.

CHAPTER 32

Nicky through A Journey of Pain

As the night draped its velvety cloak over the world, Nicky is in Marytza's hands, and Father Sébastien stays praying. Nicky's spirit is on a cross, facing punishment for disobedience. Marytza, upset, talks to Nicky, saying he is letting their family down for another girl. She wanted to marry Nicky and take care of him, but he chose someone else. She hits Nicky with a magic wand, bending his limbs, and then she and Nicky's mother hurt him. Nicky cries out in pain.

Nicky found himself ensnared in Marytza's clutches, a prisoner of her wrath. Father Sébastien, his stoic figure, remained entrenched in prayer, sensing the impending storm. His somber profile, his visage a testament to the weight of his faith. Memories intertwined, displaying fleeting encounters between him and Marytza, their destinies bound by an unseen thread. Meanwhile, Nicky's spirit languished on a metaphorical crucifix within the confines of a fractured family world, shackled by the consequences of his defiance. Punishment loomed, a specter of retribution for his transgressions. Marytza's voice, thick with resentment, pierced the suffocating silence as she berated Nicky for his betrayal. Her words carried the weight of shattered dreams, of promises unfulfilled. She had envisioned a future entwined with Nicky, a sanctuary built upon the foundation of their love. But Nicky's heart had strayed, lured by the siren song of another. Marytza's despair morphed into fury, her magic wand a conduit for her wrath. With a flick of her wrist, she unleashed her power, bending Nicky's limbs to her will.

The air crackled with tension as Nicky's cries of agony echoed off the walls, a symphony of suffering. His mother, once a paragon of tenderness, stood by Marytza's side, complicit in her son's torment. And, each blow struck a chord of betrayal, a reminder of Nicky's forsaken vows. His body bore the bruises of his folly, a testament to the price of his indiscretion.

Father Sebastian and Marytza arrived in time, interrupting Nicky's ominous ritual. As Nicky prepared to burn, the unexpected visitors brought with them an air of divine intervention. Father Sebastian, his voice resonating with authority, requested incense, invoking the sacred to counter the profane.

In response to Sebastian's request, Marytza swiftly sent forth holy water, a potent weapon against the darkness that threatened to consume them all. The albinos, once imposing in their otherworldly stature, began to crumble like saddled statues, their demise marked by a spectral spray.

With a deft hand, Marytza deciphered the cryptic codes surrounding Nicky's ritual, unlocking the mystery shrouding the sacrificial scene. Removing Nicky from the cross, she liberated him from the clutches of the infernal flame that danced below.

As they retreated from the perilous site, now tainted by the remnants of dark magic, Father Sebastian found himself unable to resist Marytza's allure. In a moment of both vulnerability and determination, he declared his personal vendetta against Nicky, thrusting his cross into one of the fallen angel's wings. With this symbolic gesture, Nicky's ability to fly was forever marred, signaling the beginning of a new conflict.

"I need your necessary evil," Father Sebastian proclaimed, his words laden with conviction and a hint of desperation, setting the stage for a battle that would test the boundaries of faith and the resilience of the human spirit.

Father Sebastien says "God after having created the sky and the earth with all that it encloses, was about to go to rest but found that an element was missing and after his superior reflection he decided to take all the remains of the good things and mixed them with all the remains of bad things from where the origin of the woman."

Father Sebastien continues by with the story of Adam's conversations with God in the Garden of Eden. "Adam said to God 'Oh God you are infinitely good, you gave me what I needed, there is only one thing I lack' and God replied 'then you will love yourself with all your heart' Adam responds 'yes, yes good and sweet lord' and God entrusted it to him. A week later, God saw the man approach who slapped and bludgeoned the companion and Adam said 'Oh Eternal Father, I was happy in the Garden of Eden, I had everything I needed and here you are giving me a cancer that is tiring me. Allow me to say with great respect that I have for you my God the evil one, which I could never have imagined, please take it back, so that I continue to live in peace, I will continue to taste the succulent fruits that you have created and amuse me incessantly with animals, my true companions.' Thus, the first of the humans could not sleep, this new creature haunted him, outside of him, inside of him, while in him raised the story of this pretty and mysterious creature; and he goes to find God and says to him 'grandfather of all time and of all centuries I'm sorry for the story I was telling you, I've come to get "the bone of my bones", I think of her, the garden has become a desert to me, the fruits have lost their flavor and the songs of the birds make me think of her with all the strength of my soul, forgive her, forgive me, forgive me I need her.' Then the voice of God said to him 'it was created from one of your ribs, protect it' and they go away. Still surprised three days later this time Adam cavalierly grabbed a strong branch from a tree and wrecked the new creature like a rundown car and the first son in order of magnitude said to God 'Oh, my good God, I blame her, I want more, deliver me from her, take it, I don't need this problem anymore.' God replied, 'If I take it back this time, you'll never see it again.' Adam reflected sighed and said 'good lord, I resign myself, it's a necessary evil.'"

Then Father Sebastian returns to Marytza whom he has atrophied, he marks his name on her with a hot iron and says "That is not my story, my 'whore', and my love despite everything, I'm seduced, I love you little filth, fruit of evil I love you despite everything." He begins to undress her to rape her and Nicky screams.

Marytza moans and Nicky too they scream so much that Nicky's guardian angel comes out of him like smoke that takes shape quickly after a woman who looks like her and the same thing happened with Marytza. Their astral now appear and surround the astral of the priest. Father Sebastian's guardian angel comes out of him and runs away and their guardian angels after a merciless struggle with the priest's astral, win the battle. Father Sebastian becomes a terracotta statue, crashed, and carried away by a turbulent wind

Through tear-streaked eyes, Nicky glimpsed the shattered remnants of his world, a tableau of broken dreams and fractured bonds. In that moment of agony, he bore the weight of his choices, the burden of his betrayal. But amidst the chaos, a flicker of resolve ignited within Nicky's soul. With each blow, with each pang of agony, he found strength anew, a beacon of defiance amidst the darkness. Lastly, for in the crucible of suffering, Nicky discovered the true measure of his resilience. He stood, battered but unbroken, ready to confront the trials that lay ahead.

CHAPTER 33

The Albino Patriarch

In a dimly lit chamber adorned with symbols of lineage and power, the albino father of Nicky beckoned to his only daughter. With an air of authority, he spoke of the solemn duty that bound their family across generations.

"Come, my only and favorite daughter," his voice resonated with a blend of pride and conviction. "Your brother has strayed from our lineage, forsaking the sacred union that ensures our purity."

Nicky, standing before him, absorbed his words with a mix of reverence and trepidation. She knew the weight of their ancestry, the expectations that rested upon her shoulders.

"He has chosen a stranger, an impure blood," her father continued, his pale features etched with disdain. "But here, in the realm of reality, our traditions endure. Brothers unite with sisters to preserve the sanctity of our race."

As he spoke, echoes of ancient customs reverberated in the chamber, reminders of a legacy steeped in tradition and superiority.

"We, like the old Jews before us, safeguard our bloodline," his voice carried a hint of reverence for their ancestors. "Our skin, unblemished and immaculate, bears witness to our purity. And with it, we wield great power over the simple earthlings who dwell below."

His words carried a sense of entitlement, a belief in the inherent superiority of their kind. To them, the world was a stage upon which they reigned supreme, orchestrating destinies, and shaping fates.

"They remain oblivious to their own folly," his tone dripped with contempt for the lesser beings. "Divided by petty conflicts, they fail to see the truth. Their struggles are our opportunities, their strife our dominion."

In the dim glow of the chamber, Nicky felt the weight of her father's expectations pressing upon her. She knew her role in their grand design, the legacy she must uphold. For theirs was a lineage forged in purity and power, a dynasty destined to endure through the ages.

CHAPTER 34

The Guardian Angels' Revelation

Nicky and Marytza stood frozen, stunned by the unexpected presence of their guardian angels. Nicky's angel, a figure shrouded in invisible yet palpable protection, revealed its eternal duty to watch over Nicky until his final breath. Marytza's angel, equally ethereal, spoke of the vast army of angels assigned to protect every soul on earth.

As the revelation sank in, Nicky and Marytza grappled with the concept of guardian angels. Were they truly surrounded by celestial beings, invisible yet ever-present? Marytza's angel posed a profound question about the nature of luck and the power of divine intervention in the face of danger.

The angels' words resonated deeply with Nicky and Marytza as they contemplated the significance of their guardians' presence. Were they merely fortunate survivors of life's trials, or were their lives guided by a higher purpose? The notion that their guardian angels could effortlessly guide them through perilous situations left them awestruck.

Nicky and Marytza began to comprehend the magnitude of their guardians' role in their lives. The angels' assurance that they could navigate even the most treacherous circumstances with ease challenged their understanding of fate and destiny. With newfound clarity, Nicky and Marytza embraced the reality of their divine protection. The tender moment of realization brought them closer together, strengthening their bond as they kissed amidst the harmonious strains of celestial music.

In the presence of their guardian angels, Nicky and Marytza surrendered to a profound sense of trust. Knowing that they were never truly alone, they found solace in the knowledge that their destinies were intertwined with the celestial realm. Nicky and Marytza gazed into each other's eyes, they saw beyond the physical realm, perceiving the invisible threads that bound them to their guardian angels. In that moment of clarity, they understood that love transcended the boundaries of mortal existence. United in their newfound understanding, Nicky and Marytza embarked on a journey guided by love and divine protection. With their guardian angels by their side, they faced the challenges of life with courage and conviction, secure in the knowledge that they were never alone.

As Nicky and Marytza embraced the mysteries of the universe, they found comfort in the presence of their guardian angels. With faith as their compass, they ventured into the unknown, ready to embrace whatever the future held. With their hearts full of gratitude and their spirits uplifted, they embarked on a journey of faith, guided by the unwavering presence of their guardian angels. In their love and trust, they found strength, knowing that they were forever cherished and protected by celestial beings beyond comprehension.

CHAPTER 35

The Garden of Forever

The sun dipped low on the horizon, casting hues of pink and gold across the sky, Nicky and Marytza strolled hand in hand through the ancient flower garden. Each step they took seemed to echo the passage of time, their love enduring like the sturdy vines that wrapped around the garden's stone archways. In this secluded oasis, where the air was thick with the perfume of a thousand blossoms, they found solace in each other's embrace. They paused beneath a canopy of roses, their laughter mingling with the gentle rustle of leaves.

As they wandered deeper into the heart of the garden, they came upon a clearing bathed in soft, golden light. Above them, a cascade of petals fell from the sky, painting the scene with vibrant splashes of color.

With a tender smile, Nicky drew Marytza close, his weathered hands cradling her face as he leaned in to kiss her. In that moment, time stood still, and they were transported to a realm where only their love existed. Around them, the garden came alive, the flowers swaying in time with the rhythm of their hearts. It was as if nature itself rejoiced in the enduring bond between Nicky and Marytza, blessing them with its eternal beauty.

As they parted, their eyes met, sparkling with a love that had only deepened with the passage of years. In that shared gaze, they found the promise of tomorrow and the memories of a lifetime lived together. With a contented sigh, they continued their journey through the garden, their footsteps echoing in harmony with the gentle melody of the wind. Hand in hand, they walked, knowing that if they had each other, they would always find paradise in the garden of their love.

And so, as the stars began to twinkle overhead, Nicky and Marytza remained, their love a beacon of light in the darkness, guiding them through the endless expanse of time. They got very old as they walked together holding hands in the beautiful flower garden, a place as romantic as the Garden of Eden. In the background, flowers fell like rain while they shared a loving kiss.

About The Author

Realph Saintil is a business coach, capital organizer, developer, and author, as well as the founder of Promoculture and Intelegenciainc.com. Known for his entrepreneurial spirit, multicultural competency and multilingual expertise, Saintil has worked extensively across corporate governance and Afro-Caribbean communities. He is a clinical educator with the New York City department of education and was appointed as an independent consultant for National Haitian American Elected Officials Network (NHAEON) and Yele Haiti's Diaspora Network, and Sounds of Tomorrow to name a few.

A dedicated leader, Saintil has spearheaded numerous initiatives, including his involvement in Brooklyn's political landscape and Haitian-American cultural projects. His novel Money, Love and Power is a testament to his deep connection to Haiti, blending history, culture, and personal insight to celebrate the richness and complexities of Haitian life. Saintil is currently pursuing a Ph.D. at Fordham University.

www.ingramcontent.com/pod-product-compliance
Lightning Source LLC
Chambersburg PA
CBHW010406310726
48979CB00012B/2144/J